GOING
FOR THE
RECORD

GOING
FOR THE
RECORD

JULIE A. SWANSON

EERDMANS BOOKS FOR YOUNG READERS

GRAND RAPIDS, MICHIGAN

Text © 2004 Julie A. Swanson
First edition 2004
This edition 2021

Published in the United States in 2021
by Eerdmans Books for Young Readers,
an imprint of Wm. B. Eerdmans Publishing Co.
Grand Rapids, Michigan

www.eerdmans.com/youngreaders

Manufactured in the United States

29 28 27 26 25 24 23 22 21   1 2 3 4 5 6 7 8 9

ISBN 978-08028-5273-2

The Library of Congress has cataloged the original edition of this book as follows:

Library of Congress Cataloging-in-Publication Data

Swanson, Julie A.
Going for the record / written by Julie A. Swanson.
p. cm.
Summary: Seventeen-year-old Leah's chance to make the U.S.
national soccer team does not seem so important when she learns
that her father has cancer and may only have months to live.
ISBN 978-0-8028-5268-8 (paper ; alk. Paper)
[1. Cancer:Fiction. 2. Soccer:Fiction. 3. Fathers and daughters:Fiction.] I. Title.
PZ7.S9717Go 2004
[Fic] — dc22
2003013031

For my Pops, Ronald Jude Polakowski, and my mom, Carol, who was every bit as inspirational before, during, and after his death. And for my grandma Helen, who has always been our family's Rock.

—J.A.S

CHAPTER 1

Friday, June 20

This must be what it feels like after you win a battle in war, or reach the summit of Mt. Everest, or give birth to a baby. The part in my hair is burnt. My feet are blistered. Everything in between is sore. I'm tired and I stink, but I've never felt better.

Last year I could barely keep from crying in front of everybody, walking across this soccer field to the parking lot. I was one of the lowly who got cut and sent home. I skittered across this field fast as I could, head down. This year, I'm one of the lucky twenty who made the Region II U-18 ODP team, and I'm taking my time, limping my way slowly towards some shade.

Gram says all those letters and numbers sound like Greek to her, and I always have to explain—the Region II U-18 ODP team is the Olympic Developmental Program's team for the best soccer players in the Midwest region of the country under eighteen. I guess it is a mouthful.

Walking across midfield, I stop. This is one of those scenes I want to preserve forever: ODP camp, summer before my senior year. I turn a slow three-sixty, soaking it in. Pony-tailed girls in their silky uniforms, red and blue jerseys, baggy white shorts. Six green velvet fields, crisply lined in white.

I start walking again, towards the trees by the parking lot. I

1

know it sounds stupid, but I feel kind of heroic in my limp. It's the closest I've ever come to a strut. All the girls nod as I pass. Even Bree Holland congratulates me. Imagine that. I've finally earned some respect down here.

From now on when people see me walking down the street they won't say, "There goes that girl . . . what's her name?" They'll say, "There goes that soccer player, Leah Weiczynkowski." And, for once, they'll know how to pronounce it: Wee-zin-kowski. Traverse City is a small town. If you get your name in the *Record Eagle*, most of the locals will have heard of you.

I imagine the guys at the restaurant sitting at the bar, placing bets on which scholarship offer I'll take—Notre Dame, North Carolina, Virginia . . .

I can't wait to go home. It's been a great week, but I've had enough of Ann Arbor. Get me back to my lake. And my bed. I could sleep for days.

Plopping down under a tree—oh, it's good to get off my feet—I pry off my cleats and peel down my socks. My toes are pickled, their tips molded squarely together. I wiggle them unstuck and rip off my shin guards. Bruises spot my legs from the knees down. I don't know why I even bother to wear them. All they give me is a bad tan.

I'd be truly comfortable now if I could just take this shirt off. My IWBTBWSPITW shirt. I got it in seventh grade when we were on vacation in Florida. I had it made up at one of those T-shirt shops. I picked out a shirt in Traverse City Trojan gold and asked the sales woman to iron on the letters IWBTB-

2

WSPITW across the chest, in black. I didn't tell her what it meant and she didn't ask. But Mom and Dad did. "What do those letters stand for, honey?" asked Mom.

IWBTBWSPITW stands for I Will Be The Best Women's Soccer Player In The World, but I wasn't telling. "I don't want to say," I said.

"Well, if you're going to wear that shirt, you'd better expect people are going to ask what it means," said Dad. "You're going to get a lot of questions about it."

I hadn't thought of that. Guess I won't be wearing it much, I remember thinking. It would have to be my secret shirt, something to wear under my jersey on cold days.

Well, I ended up wearing it for every game. Five years in a row now.

It's pretty tattered. The gold has faded and the letters are peeling up. It's been washed and dried so many times it fits like a cropped Lycra top. But that's okay. It's less noticeable under my jersey now. I wear it inside out under whites so the letters won't show through. I'm not trying to make a statement to anyone with it, just to myself.

I love this shirt.

Come on, Dad. Come on.

I watch the other girls greet their parents, and it strikes me funny how many different kinds of hugs I see.

Lots of I'm-so-proud-of-you-anyway hugs.

A dad's giant bear hug that lifts the girl right off the ground.

Maggie Burns—she made it to the final pool of twenty-five before she got cut—she just buries her face in her mom's neck.

3

That was me last year.

Then there's the mad, stiff, pulling away hug. This is so unfair. All politics. Get me out of here.

Bree Holland's dad slaps her on the rump like a football coach. This is old hat for them.

I wonder what my dad will do. He's going to be so excited. Come on, Dad. Come on.

Everyone's gone now. It's just me under this tree and a couple of staff coaches sitting in a golf cart across the field. I think they're waiting for me.

This isn't like Dad; he's never late. I've been sitting here in this sweat-drenched shirt so long I'm actually getting cold.

I'm just about to strip down to my sports bra and go sit in the sun—I could warm up and get rid of this farmer's tan at the same time—when Coach Sobek from the University of Michigan comes buzzing up in a golf cart.

"Leah? Do you have a ride?"

"Yeah, my dad's coming." Dad's my chauffeur. I got my driver's license last year, but I don't have my own car. He insists on driving me. He enjoys it. He tries out all the restaurants along the way, looking for ideas.

Dad loves watching me play, too. I think he kind of lives through me. Mom says he was a good athlete in high school— he's still a great golfer—but my brother and sister never amounted to much in sports, so he was glad when I came along to show what kind of genes he'd passed down.

Sometimes I hear him bragging about me in his restaurant. "She's the toughest little thing you've ever seen. And fast?

She's so fast they call her Weasel, the way she darts about." It's so embarrassing.

Coach Sobek drives back to the other coach. They both look down at their watches and talk for a minute. I look towards the parking lot. Still empty.

"Leah," calls Coach Sobek, buzzing back over to me, "why don't you climb in? I'll give you a ride up to the dorms so you can call home and find out if your dad's on his way."

"Oh, he's coming. You don't have to wait here with me."

"Yes, I do. We can't leave you. Where's your dad coming from?"

"Home. Traverse City." It's a five-hour drive.

"Well, maybe he got stuck in traffic. I tell you what. We'll wait here another ten minutes, and if he doesn't show I'll take you up to the dorms."

"Okay."

What can I say? I am starting to worry now.

"You had a great week, Leah," says Coach Sobek.

"Thanks," I say, blushing stupidly.

"There were quite a few college coaches here today. Your phone's going to be ringing off the hook." He laughs like he's beating them all to it. "What are you looking for in a school?"

"I'm looking for one that has a strong soccer program . . . "
Gently as I can, I try to tell him, no, I'm not interested in U of M. It's a great school, but everyone knows what a joke Coach Sobek is.

But he's persistent if nothing else. "We're an up-and-coming team at U of M. Eleven and nine last year, first time in the program's history we broke five hundred."

Right, with all those wins coming against a bunch of pansy non-conference teams. They lost every single game in the Big Ten.

"And this year we've got all our starters coming back. But of course you could come in and play right away, Leah, and I'd have to bench one of them." He lets loose a dirty laugh, and I'm glad I'm not one of those eleven starters.

"We could really use a new midfielder," he continues. "I know you play up front, but how would you feel about playing midfield? I think you'd be terrific there. Heck, you could play anywhere on the field."

He raises his eyebrows like, how about it?

I look to the parking lot, hoping Dad is there to come to my rescue.

I nod. It's easier to go along with him than to tell him the truth. Part of me is enjoying his attention, anyway. He's the first major college coach who's ever talked to me like this.

Coach Sobek takes a look at his watch. "So what do you say we take a ride up to the dorms? It's been at least ten minutes."

I get up, already stiff, and gather my stuff into my bag.

As I slide in the cart next to Coach Sobek, I take one last look over my shoulder for Dad.

The jeep!

"There he is!" I hop out of the cart and start running for Dad, a week's worth of sweaty laundry thumping against my back.

"Sorry I kept you waiting," I yell back to Coach Sobek.

"Pops!" I shout. He breaks into a tilt-headed grin. I can

6

always make him smile.

"Hey, Weez!" he says, opening the door for me. "How you doing, kiddo? Missed you."

"Pops, I did it! I made the regional team!"

His eyebrows lift over his glasses and his whole face lights into a smile.

"Well!" He reaches over and ruffles my hair. "That's my Weez! I knew you would do it this time. Give me a special on it."

I lean over and give him a kiss. He slaps me on the thigh and squeezes my knee.

"Colorado Springs, here I come!"

He's beaming, staring at me like the proudest papa ever. If I didn't know better, I'd swear he was crying, the way his face is so red and his smile all tight-lipped. I can't see through those dark glasses, though.

Dad shakes his head like he can't believe it. "So, they finally came to their senses. It's about time. Just for that I'll buy you lunch. Anything you want."

"I'm not hungry. I drank half the water cooler after our last match."

Dad shrugs. "Okay." He puts the jeep in gear. "Not even an ice cream?"

And then it occurs to me. "I'm sorry. You didn't eat yet? That's where I thought you were—gorging on some gourmet lunch and trying to squeeze the recipe out of the chef."

He doesn't even smile. "No, no. That's not what kept me."

"If you're hungry, let's stop somewhere," I say.

"No, I'm fine," he says quietly.

It isn't like Dad to play the martyr. That's Mom.

We pull out of the parking lot, stiffened by an awkward silence. I don't get it. This isn't like him at all.

We're halfway across campus and neither one of us has said a thing.

"Well, Pops, this is it," I say, trying to sound cheerful. "The first step towards the Olympics! The Notre Dame coach was there watching, too."

Dad still doesn't say anything. He's hard to read sometimes, especially with those photo grays hiding his eyes.

"Did you hear me? I said the Notre Dame coach was watching."

"No, I heard you, Weez."

"Aren't you happy? You've been dying for me to go to Notre Dame."

Dad forces a weak smile. "Yeah, I'm real happy for you, Weez."

Happy for me? We're in this together. All the trips we've taken. Driving through the night to get home. He's done it all gladly, always as excited as I am about what might come of it.

Dad doesn't take his eyes off the road, not even at the stoplight.

"What then, Pops?"

"It's just that I have some bad news. That's why I'm late. I've been driving around thinking about how I'm going to tell you."

"Tell me what?" Mom isn't going to make me go to the family reunion and miss Colorado Springs, is she?

"Leah."

He only uses my real name when he's dead serious. Maybe the restaurant lost its liquor license—

"I have cancer."

It knocks the wind out of me. From the inside out, a coldness seeps through my body, as if something at my very core has burst and is releasing itself, like one of those first-aid cool packs.

I stare at him, open-mouthed; he won't even look at me.

"I haven't been feeling too well, terrible stomach pains. So I went in for a checkup. And they found cancer."

He says it so matter-of-factly.

"I didn't know you weren't feeling well."

"Remember the stomachache I had on the way down here?"

"You said it was from the Big Macs we ate."

"It got worse, wouldn't go away. It got so bad I couldn't sleep that night. Your mom made me go see the doctor the next day."

"But you're not going to die." Surely he's going to tell me no, that they caught it early and it's a highly treatable form of cancer.

"We all die, Weez."

"I know, but you're not going to die on account of this. It's not like the doctor gave you so many months to live or anything, right?"

"Three."

"Three? Three what?" I ask, my skin prickling with goose

bumps.

"Three months to live. I have pancreatic cancer. There's no cure. The doctor says it's the fastest kind. It's already spread to my liver."

My teeth start chattering, my knees knocking together, my elbows vibrating against my ribs.

"Well, maybe the doctor's wrong!" I blurt out. "You look fine. You don't look sick at all. You're too young. It's not fair!" I can't tell if I'm screaming or mouthing the words. My ears are ringing. And I'm cold, so cold.

CHAPTER 2

Dad pulls over. He hugs me for a long time. Rocks me back and forth.

When I stop shaking I peel his arms off and put my head in his lap. I lay there, crying softly. Dad smoothes my hair back, over and over.

We don't say anything. Cars whiz by on the highway. A semi roars past, its wind shaking us.

Finally I'm done. I get up and wipe my eyes and stare out my window. I don't feel cold anymore, just numb.

Dad starts up the jeep and gets back on the highway.

"Come on," he says quietly, offering me his hand, "let's go for the record."

When I was little, I used to hold Dad's hand all the time. Walking, driving, sitting next to him in church. When I got too old for it, he teased me about it. He'd keep putting his hand out and say, "Well, aren't you going to hold my hand? What's the matter? Think you're too old? Come on." And he'd grab for my hand. He still does that. He'll try to be sneaky and reach over when I'm not looking, but I'll catch him out the corner of my eye and pull my hand away.

"Oh, come on," he'll say, "let's go for the record. You like to break records. You broke the state scoring record, didn't you?

Let's see if you can set a new one and hold my hand all the way home. You've never done that before."

"Cut it out, Dad," I moan. "You're not even funny. Just drive."

Going for the record. It's a standing joke now. I can always count on his hand sliding across the seat at some point. I see it coming and shake my head. Once in a while, if I'm in a really great mood, I'll slap him five and he'll be satisfied with that and leave me alone for the rest of the ride.

Seeing Dad's hand palm up on the seat between us, I slip my mine into his. Today I'll go for the record with him.

It's been a long silence, but not an empty one. Dad and I exchange looks, even smiles. We squeeze each other's hands.

"Can't they operate and take it out?"

Dad shakes his head.

"No chemotherapy or radiation?"

"No. The doctor says there are experimental things we could try, but nothing that's got a very good track record."

"But you're going to try the experimental stuff, right?"

"I don't know."

"You don't know?" My jaw drops. Dad buys a lottery ticket every day. He bets on golf, football, basketball, baseball, the Kentucky Derby. Why isn't he willing to gamble now, when he has everything to gain and nothing to lose?

"Why not?" I almost shout it at him.

"Well," Dad sighs, his grip tightening on the steering wheel, "before I'd jump into anything, I'd need to know what it would involve, where I'd have to go for treatments, what the side effects would be."

"Where you'd go? The side effects? Who cares? What could possibly be worse than dying?"

"Weez, even if experimental treatments could buy me time, the doctor says we'd be talking weeks or months, not years. If I've only got a short time to live, I might as well enjoy it and be at home with you rather than lying in some hospital bed hooked up to a machine."

"Stop it, Dad. Don't talk like that. You act like it's a done deal." My nose stings; I'm going to cry again. I turn and look out the window.

"You might not want to hear it," says Dad, "but you need to. You need to understand. I'd rather spend sixty good days with you than live for six more months and put us all through hell. I'd have to go downstate for treatments. That's a lot of traveling, a lot of time, and a lot of money. Insurance won't pay for anything experimental. It's going to be enough of a drain on the family emotionally; I don't want to put us under financially, too."

Financially? How can he talk like this? How can he put a dollar and cent value on his life?

"Doctors can be wrong, Dad. You should get a second opinion."

"I did."

That settles that, I guess. I deflate into the seat.

"Well, sort of," Dad admits. "Dr. Michaels suspected it was cancer when I first went in. He sent me to a specialist who

13

confirmed the diagnosis, and he gave me the name of three other specialists I could go to for second opinions. But he said I have a classic case, all the signs and symptoms."

"What signs? What symptoms? Besides a stomachache."

"It's a bad stomachache, Weez. And I've lost a lot of weight."

"I thought you were on a diet."

"Shoot, everyone's on a diet when they're my age. But I haven't been eating any less than I ever do."

"Maybe it's all the golf you've been playing this summer."

"I always play this much golf. Listen, they aren't just going by the stomach pains and the weight loss. I'm jaundiced, too."

I look hard at Dad—his face, his hands, his legs sticking out of his shorts. He's brown as a nut, Gram would say, healthy-looking as ever.

Dad sees me examining him. "The doctor said it's hard to notice when you have a tan. He saw it in my eyes." Dad pulls his glasses down his nose. "See how the whites have yellowed?"

Sure enough. It's no wonder none of us ever noticed it, though; he's always wearing those stupid glasses. Dad and his photo grays. He wears them all the time, inside and out.

Paul used to tease him, "Who do you think you are, Dad, a movie star? Buy yourself some regular glasses and save these for outside."

"I'm in and out of the restaurant all day long," Dad would argue. "I can't be fidgeting around for another pair of glasses every time I go outside. Besides, they lighten up indoors."

"Not enough they don't," Paul would say, and he's right;

even at their lightest, the lenses are brown like iced tea.

"Okay," I say to Dad, "so you have stomachaches, you've lost weight, and you're jaundiced. How do they know that means you have cancer?"

"Weez," Dad says in a real tired voice, "they've done tests to confirm it. Blood tests, needle biopsies, ultrasounds. They know it's cancer."

"We've got to stop by the restaurant on the way home," Dad says when we hit Chums Corners. It's the first thing he's said since Cadillac.

"Why?" I just want to get home.

"Your mom wants me to pick up dinner. It'll only take a minute."

I cough a sigh at him. His stops at the restaurant take forever. I can't believe he's in the mood to see anyone. I'm certainly not. Flipping up the visor mirror, I see that my eyes are as swollen and bloodshot as they feel. "I'll wait in the car."

"Come on in, Weez. You look fine."

"Oh, all right." I unbuckle and follow him in.

Pushing through the restaurant's double doors, the Grand Pooh-Bah enters his domain. He's so funny, the way he moves. It's not really a strut or a swagger, but it's proud, almost cocky in its coolness, its slowness no matter what the rush. He's like a float going by in a parade.

"How do you like what we did while you were gone?" Dad hollers back to me over the murmur of voices and clink of china, pointing out the freshly painted woodwork.

I lean against a pillar and watch him. You'd never know that there's anything wrong with him. He's weaving in and out among the tables, patting backs, shaking hands, waving and smiling.

He looks good. With his potbelly gone, I notice how straight he stands. Except for the gray hair, he looks like he did when he was thirty. And I'm struck by his jaw line. When he was heavier, his face tapered into the thickness of his neck, and I never noticed it. He looks really handsome tonight.

I bet they're wrong. I bet he's fine.

"Hey, Leah!" A yell comes from behind the swinging kitchen doors.

I go back and say hi to Kristin and the rest of the dishwashing crew. Enzo's there, too. He's hilarious. He fits right in with these kids. He's fifty going on fifteen with his shaggy hair and his jeans sliding down his butt.

"How're you doing?" Kristin yells over the hand-held sprayer she's waving. "I haven't seen you since before school let out." Kristin plays goalie on our high school team. We're going to be co-captains this year.

"I know," I yell back to Kristin. "I just got back from ODP camp."

"Yeah? How'd it go?"

"Good. Really good." I don't feel like talking, but I don't want to seem like a snob. "What've you been up to?"

Kristin holds up her yellow-gloved hands. "Right here, making money. I'm taking a week off next month to go to soccer camp at Central, though."

"Good for you!" I know that's what she wants to hear. A whole week of camp is more than most of the players on our team will do.

"Yeah, I've got to get these hands and feet ready. Nobody gets by us unless the ball gets past me."

"Come on, Kristin." I say, warming up now. "You know the sad truth. Goalies never win games for you, but they sure can lose them."

"Shut up, Leah!" She laughs and flings a handful of suds at me. "Get out of here before your dad fires me. I've got work to do."

"When's your old man going to put you to work?" asks Enzo. He hikes up his pants and slicks back his hair, challenging me. Enzo loves to spar.

I blush. Not because of what he thinks—Enzo's been with us ever since I can remember; he's like an uncle to me—but because of the other people here.

"Enzo," I tease him back for everyone to hear, "you know I'm the fill-in girl. I only work when one of you gets sick. Otherwise, I hang around eating up the profits and watching European soccer on the big screen in the bar."

You see, that's Enzo. He washes dishes, cooks, waits tables, runs errands, and does whatever else Dad needs. And he loves soccer. He and his buddies live for their Saturday pick-up games.

"Must be nice." Enzo pretends I'm really talking about myself.

17

"Somebody's got to be available. Besides, I'm busy with soccer." I get a little bit serious in case the others don't know we're teasing.

Enzo winks. "You don't have to do no explaining to me. I know you got things going. I see how you run your old man ragged with all the chasing around after you he does."

I try to smile because I really like Enzo. He didn't mean anything by that.

"Come on, Weez." Dad sweeps by carrying a stack of carryout containers in one hand and a white bag in the other. "Let's get this food home to your mother while it's still hot."

CHAPTER 3

Mom runs down the back steps like she's been watching for us. She looks terrible. Her hair's a mess. There are dark circles under her eyes. She doesn't say anything, just hugs me and makes lots of gulpy, swallowing noises.

We go inside, the three of us, arm in arm, and sit on the couch. Mom and Dad go to reach for each other and, being that their inside arms are stuck around my shoulders, I'm drawn into a three-way embrace with them. We sit, heads together, saying nothing. Then Mom and Dad start crying.

Maybe it's because I had a big cry a couple hours ago, but I feel rather indifferent to it all. I'm just sitting here holding up these two adults. It's weird; for the first time in my life I feel stronger than my parents. I've only seen Dad cry once before, the day Paul went away to college.

"Well, Leah," Mom finally says, sniffling into a Kleenex she's pulled from her sleeve, "you know our news. Let's hear yours. How was your week?"

We all sit back.

"It was good. I made the regional team. Big deal, huh?"

Mom and Dad burst out laughing.

"Oh, it feels so good to laugh!" cries Mom, dabbing her eyes. "Seriously, though, Leah, congratulations. I'm sorry you can't enjoy your accomplishment like you might have."

"Yeah, we sure got thrown a curve ball." Everything's a cliché to Dad.

"Speaking of baseball, where's Gram?" I ask.

"Back in her room," says Mom. "Why don't you go and see her."

Gram's head is bent low over a newspaper crossword puzzle and she's listening, as usual, to the crackly broadcast of a Brewer's game on her radio.

"Hi, Gram."

She peers up over her glasses. "Well, look who's home. Our little nomad."

I force a smile.

"So you know about your pa." Gram pats the end of her bed for me to sit down.

"Brewers are up nine to one in the eighth. They've got the game all sewed up," she says, turning the radio off. "Here, sweetie, have some nusheri." Using her foot, she hooks a plastic container of pistachios and pulls it out from under the bed. I don't feel like any, but I pick it up anyway.

"I can't believe it about Dad," I say. "I wish it was one of his stupid April Fools jokes." Once he fell off of his chair and lay motionless on the floor. Mom did CPR on him until he couldn't keep a straight face any longer.

"I too, I too," Gram says softly, shaking her head.

"What are we going to do, Gram?" My voice cracks.

"We're going to storm heaven, that's what we're going to

20

do." She pounds her fist on the arm of her stuffed chair. "We'll pray and we'll pray and we'll pray until Jesus gets so sick of hearing us that he says, 'Okay, okay, I'll do it. I'll make him better.'"

"I knew I could count on you, Gram!" I lean over and give her a hug. "I mean, no matter what the doctors say, there's always hope, right?"

"That's right. Them folks on the talk shows, they beat the odds all the time. No reason your pa can't be like them."

"I wish they believed that."

"What do you mean, they? Who?"

"Mom and Dad. It's like they've already given up."

"Oh, sweetie, they're in shock. Give them time. Your dad's a fighter. If anyone can beat this, he can."

I'm staring down at the pistachios, not wanting her to see that I'm not so sure.

"Penny for your thoughts?"

I can't lie to Gram. I raise my head and look at her. "I was just thinking, what if. What if Dad does die?"

"You dasn't talk like that!" Gram shakes a finger at me. "Don't let them thoughts enter your mind, much less come out your mouth. Prayers don't do no good if you haven't got faith in our Lord's power to deliver on them."

"Take these nuts out and share them with your mom and dad," Gram orders me. "It's time for me to say my rosary."

I'm walking down the hall with the pistachios when Mom yells, "Leah, Telephone!"

21

She's standing in the kitchen with her hand over the receiver, grinning. "It's Clay," she whispers, making her eyebrows dance.

It's so stupid. Just because Clay and I hang out together Mom thinks we're in love. It's all wishful thinking on her part. She's always telling me how she started dating when she was thirteen. She can't seem to understand that I have no interest.

"Hi, Clay," I say, flashing a steely glare at Mom. She goes away, but not out of eavesdropping range; I can hear her spangly bracelets jingling in the pantry.

"Welcome home, partner! How'd it go?" It's good to hear his voice.

"I made the regional team."

"All right! I knew you would. See? All that work we did paid off. And you have nobody but me, your personal trainer, to thank."

Clay plays soccer, too. He's not that good, but being a guy, he's stronger and faster, so he's a great training partner.

"I know. What would I do without you?" I say.

"Hey, do you want to go for a run? I was such a slouch while you were gone."

"No, I'm really tired."

"You, tired? What? Can it be? We're talking about the famous Weasel Weiczynkowski."

"Shut up, Clay."

"No, really! I've never heard you talk like that. Are you okay?"

"I'm fine."

22

"Do you want to do something else, then? Go swimming? Waterskiing? I could drive over in the boat and pick you up in five minutes."

Clay lives on the peninsula. You can see his house across the water from our living room window.

"Nah, we're about to eat dinner."

"What about later tonight?"

"I don't know. I'm really tired." I look around; Mom's still within hearing distance. "How about I give you a call after dinner? Maybe I'll feel better by then."

Dinner is weird. After we pray — the same old "Bless Us, Oh Lord" we always rattle off — it's like nobody knows what to say.

Gram breaks the ice. "The Brewers won today. Nine to one."

"Did they, Ma?" says Dad. "That's good. Who'd they play?"

"The Red Sox."

Dad nods.

Mom clears her throat. "Would anyone like a roll?"

"So Paul and Mary are coming up," says Dad, taking a roll.

"Yes. They'll both be here for dinner tomorrow night," says Mom.

I freeze, a forkful of food about to enter my open mouth. They both live downstate, a good five hours away; they rarely come to visit unless it's a holiday.

"Paul and Mary know?" I say. "When did they find out?"

"Oh, I don't know. We called them pretty much right away."

"So they've known for almost a week and you're just now telling me?"

"We didn't want to interrupt your camp," says Mom. "It would have spoiled the week for you."

"Who cares? My whole year is spoiled! What would another week have mattered?" I'm trying not to yell. "You should have told me right away!"

"Oh, Leah."

"No, really. I might be the baby of the family, but you don't have to spare me. I can take it. I can handle it."

"Listen, I'm sorry," says Mom. "Maybe we should have told you sooner."

"Maybe? Wouldn't you have wanted to know right away?"

"Okay, okay. I'm sorry. From now on we'll be sure to tell you as soon as we know something. I promise."

Normally Dad doesn't let me speak that way to Mom, but he hasn't said a word.

"You should give your brothers a call tonight, Pete," Mom says to Dad.

"Why?"

"Well, if this is how Leah reacts—"

"That's right," says Gram. "I wasn't going to say anything, but," she points her finger at Dad, "you'd want to know if one of them was sick."

Dad gets on the phone right after dinner.

"Hey, Al." Uncle Al is Dad's oldest brother. He has five, and when there's big news, he always calls them in order, oldest to youngest. So I know there are four more calls after this one.

I go out into the living room and turn on the TV. Even if I

don't want to hear what Dad is saying, I will anyway. Our house is open between the kitchen, dining room, and living room, and Dad talks really loud. Sometimes I wish he had a dial on his chest and I could go over and turn his volume down.

"How're you doing, Al? . . . Me? Well, I haven't been feeling too sharp. . . . Stomach pains. Got so bad I finally went in for a checkup . . . Thought it was an intestinal bug, but I'll be damned if the doctor didn't tell me it was cancer."

He's bellowing it out like they're discussing a Packer's game, and he's strolling around like he does when he cruises the restaurant, shoulders back, chest out, gut sucked in, as if Uncle Al can see him. "No, they don't have to operate . . . Chemo? I don't know. I've got an appointment with the doctor Monday. I'll know more then. Hey, it's not as bad as it sounds. Besides a twinge now and then, I feel fine."

Liar.

"Don't worry. I'm a tough old dog. I'll beat this thing," says Dad.

I can't believe my ears. I'm glad to hear it, but does he really believe it? Or is he just saying it to make Uncle Al feel better?

Dad calls Uncle Jerry, Uncle Keith, Uncle Frank, and Uncle Joey, saying the same things over and over, trying to sound upbeat. When he's finished he takes his glasses off and sits down in a heap at the dining room table, rubbing his eyes, totally spent.

I take the cordless phone into my bedroom.

"Clay? Sorry. My dad's been on the phone all night. I know it's too late to go out in the boat, but do you want to get some ice cream?"

"Sure. I'll pick you up." Clay has his own car. He got it for his sixteenth birthday, the brat.

"I'll meet you at the end of the driveway," I say.

"Whatever." Clay knows I'm weird about having him over. He doesn't say anything about it anymore, but it used to bug him. If we're just friends, he'd say, why do you care what your parents think? I know, I'd say, but I hate how my mom watches us, and, my dad'll tease me about it even though he knows there's nothing to it.

I put on my running shoes so it looks like I'm going jogging. I don't want them to think Clay's taking me out on a date.

"Mom? Dad? I'm going out for a while," I yell.

Mom comes twinkle toeing out from her bedroom. "Oh, honey, you're not going running, are you? Give yourself a rest."

"I'm stiff, Mom. I've got to loosen up my legs."

"Honestly, Leah, I think you're addicted to it. You're obsessed with soccer."

Addicted, obsessed. She spits the words out like venom.

She shakes her head. "A girl your age should be more well-rounded and not spend every spare moment working out. You should go to parties. Go shopping. Hang out with girlfriends. And what about boyfriends?"

I can't believe it. It actually feels good to get her old lecture on overdoing it. It's the first time since Dad picked me up in

Ann Arbor that anything's felt normal.

"It's not healthy, Leah. You can't eat, drink, and sleep soccer. Back me up on this, Pete. Don't you think she should take it easy?"

"Your mother's right," says Dad. "Keep this up and pretty soon you'll be pooping little soccer balls." But he winks at me; he's the same way about golf. Still, his pooping-little-soccer-balls irritates me.

"Ha, ha, Dad." It's not that he thinks he's clever that gets me. It's that he says it just to satisfy Mom. What about me? Why doesn't he ever back me up?

I hate it when Mom says I'm obsessed. Like I'm a psycho. But, hey, I don't care. There's nothing more important to me than my goal, and it's paid off. Most mothers would be delighted if their kid earned a free college education.

"I'll take it easy, Mom, I promise."

"Leah, the sun's about to set. I don't want you out there alone at night, and you know that. I'm afraid I'm going to have to put my foot down."

That does it. She always pushes me to this point. "Don't worry, Mom. I won't be alone. I'm going with Clay."

"All right, but stay where it's well-lit. Don't go off—"

"We won't!" I say, and I'm out the door, running. Each step kills. My muscles are raw meat. But this is what I said I was going to do, and I know Mom is watching out the window.

Clay is waiting at the mailbox in his black Lexus. He's got this big grin and looks as fresh as a peach, but then it all drops away when he sees me up close.

"Whoa, you do look tired. Your eyes."

"It's been a long week. A long day."

"You okay?"

I shrug. "Been better." I can't fake happiness tonight.

"What's wrong?"

I start to cry and feel so stupid. I've only cried in front of Clay once, when I sprained my ankle. But never because I was upset. I get hurt, mad, frustrated, but I don't get emotional. Not like some girls.

"What is it, Leah? Did you get in a fight with your mom? She's not going to let you go to national camp?"

I shake my head and wave for him to go. Drive, just drive.

Instead of going to Borden's for ice cream he takes us to East Bay beach. Which is fine with me. I'm a mess, and the sunset's better at West Bay, so hardly anyone comes to East Bay this time of evening.

As soon as the car comes to a stop, I get out and walk down towards the water. Clay will follow me; I know he will.

"Are you going to tell me what's wrong, or do I have to keep guessing?" Clay says from behind me. I stop and sit cross-legged in the sand. Clay sits down facing me, and I tell him everything.

I don't know how long it's taken to get it all out, but it's almost dark, and I'm a snotty mess.

"Promise not to tell anyone? Because Dad doesn't want anyone but family to know right now."

"I promise," says Clay, moving so he's sitting beside me now. "I'm sorry. So sorry. I don't know what else to say."

I start crying again, softly this time, under control. I'm just starting to feel really peaceful—glad that I told Clay and that I've got a friend like him here with me—when he puts his arm around me.

"Don't," I say, pulling away. "I'm gross. Look at my shirt."

Clay gives me one of his little I-can't-believe-you coughs, crosses his arms over his knees, and stares out at the lights across the bay.

"I think we better get going," I say. "I don't want my mom to worry."

Mom's there to greet me when I get home. My loyal watchdog. She's so excited to see me, she's practically panting.

"You got some phone calls while you were out. One was from Coach Kenney. He wants to know how your week went and whether you can make it to practice on Wednesday instead of Thursday. You're supposed to call him. And several college coaches called. I can't remember where they said they're—"

"—Clemson, Notre Dame, Harvard, and Wisconsin," Dad barks.

Wow. Coach Sobek was right. I didn't think it would happen this fast though.

"What'd they say? What'd you tell them?"

"They wanted to talk to you, of course, but I told them you were out for a run." Mom smiles this silly grin, all proud of herself for saying something that might get me a few bonus points. "They're going to call you again tomorrow."

Great. So now I've got to hang around the house tomorrow

dreading those phone calls.

"Weez?" Dad calls to me as I walk down the hall towards my bedroom. "When you talk to Coach Kenney tell him you'll be there for practice on Wednesday. Nothing's changed; I'm still your chauffeur."

I often forget to say my bedtime prayers, but not tonight. Please, God, bless Dad. Please, Jesus, bless him. Please bless my dad. Please bless Dad, please bless Dad, please bless Dad. I'm storming heaven, just like Gram said we should.

The moon's coming up right outside the window over my bed. It's big and round over the trees, and the woods are full of slanty moon shadows striping the ground. You wouldn't even need a flashlight out there tonight, it's so bright.

It's really eerie in here with these rectangular shafts of blue-white light beaming in over my bed. They cut such a low angle they're almost parallel to the ground. Telescoping as they cross the room, they fall like spotlights on my Wall of Fame.

It's been a long time since I took a good look at that wall. Paul made up the name—Wall of Fame. He makes fun of it. "Nothing like celebrating yourself," he says.

But it's the one un-modest thing I've allowed myself, and it isn't a braggy display or anything. It's in the privacy of my own bedroom, on the wall you can't see when you look in the door. My plaques, medals, and framed awards hang on the wall. My trophies and game balls sit on the shelf over them.

These are my prized possessions, my treasures: Most Valuable Camper, All-Conference, Single-Season Scoring

Record, All-State, Player of the Year, All-American.

And now I've got another honor to add to my collection: Region II U-18 ODP Team. They didn't give us a trophy or anything, but we had our picture taken. I'm going to frame it.

CHAPTER 4

Saturday, June 21

"Leah," Mom says, shaking me. "Honey, wake up."

I crack an eye and squint at the alarm clock. It's only ten-thirty. "Just give me a couple more hours, Mom, please." I could sleep until dinner.

"I would, honey, but the Notre Dame coach is on the phone for you."

I tear out to the kitchen and by the time I get there I'm practically hyperventilating.

"Hello?" I manage to spit out fairly normally, and then I quickly cover the receiver so she can't hear how loud I'm breathing.

"Hi, Leah. This is Coach McNall from Notre Dame. Sorry to get you out of bed. I should have known you'd be tired after the week you had."

"Oh, no, no, no, it's okay. I should be up anyway."

"Listen, I saw you play in Ann Arbor, and I was really impressed. Congratulations on making the regional team."

"Thanks."

"Do you have any interest in the University of Notre Dame?"

"Yeah. I mean, yes. Yes, I do."

"Good, because we're very interested in you. We'd like to

invite you for an official visit in September."

September. The month Dad's supposed to die. I flush hot all over. "Well, our high school cards aren't printed up yet. I don't know when our games are."

"Tell you what. Why don't you talk to your coach and find out. Get back to me soon as you know something. We'll set something up then."

"All right."

"It's been good talking to you. I'm looking forward to meeting you."

"Me, too."

"You take care, Leah. And again, congratulations."

"Okay, thanks. Bye."

What a mess. All these coaches will be calling with the same questions, and I won't be able to give them a straight answer to anything.

I think I'll go running. Or to Clay's house. Anything to stay away from the phone.

When Paul arrives, slung low in his new gold Porsche convertible, my first instinct is to run out to him, but I hold back. I don't want to look too eager. He already has such an inflated opinion of himself.

I watch him unfold his body from the car, looking like he just stepped off the cover of GQ: shiny black shoes, creased dress pants, starched white shirt with the collar unbuttoned, tie loosened. He pushes his sunglasses up into his tousled black curls and looks around. Now I run out.

"Hi, you, kiddo!" He picks me up and twirls me around.

"Pauly!" Gram hurries out the front door, followed by Mom and Dad.

"I couldn't get here fast enough," he says. "I did about ninety miles an hour the whole way."

Mom kisses and hugs him, eyes closed, hanging on tight.

Dad shakes his hand and whacks him on the back.

"Tell me what I can do to help while I'm here," Paul says. "Really, anything. I'll cut the grass, chop wood. Heck, I'll even tend bar at the restaurant."

We're still standing in the driveway when Mary and Hugh pull up.

"Daddy!" Waddling with her arms outstretched and her face contorted by emotion, Mary looks like a little kid pretending to be a monster. When she reaches Dad her huge, pregnant belly hits first and she topples over at the waist, collapsing into him.

"Daddy," she sobs. "Oh, Daddy, I'm so scared."

Dad looks uncomfortable trying to hold Mary up. He works to get himself out from under her wrap and transfers her over to Mom. Mary's oblivious to it. With Mary draped over Mom now, Hugh shakes Dad's hand, patting him awkwardly on the back, like he's too fragile to take the hearty whack usually exchanged among the males in our family.

We sit on the deck and eat hors d'oeuvres while Dad barbecues steaks for dinner. Mary talks endlessly about the baby. And all the while I'm doing isometrics, working my quads and hams.

Isometrics are cool. You just sit there, tightening and holding opposing muscles groups, invisibly building up strength. You can smile and talk while you're doing it, and no one will ever know.

And Mom says I'm addicted. She doesn't know the half of it.

"Have you picked out names yet?" asks Paul. "I mean, besides Paul."

"Very funny," says Mary. "For a girl we like Emily Rose or Laura Jane. For a boy we're leaning towards a—a family name."

"What's the due date, Mary?

"September seventh."

Less than three months. In my mind I see a calendar, the date circled in red. It will give Dad something to shoot for, a reason to fight.

"So, Leah," says Paul, "what's next for you and soccer?"

"I'm not sure."

"Oh, yes, you are," Dad barks. "I'm still your chauffeur. I can drive just fine. You'll be going to practices, and you'll be going to the Fourth of July tournament, and you'll be going to the national camp in August."

"Honey, we haven't settled that yet," Mom interrupts. "The national camp is the same week as the family reunion."

"Mumma," says Dad, "she's worked so hard for this."

"I don't want to argue about it right now," says Mom.

"No, we need to talk about it," insists Dad. "If she's going to go, I've got to book her a flight. You know how hard it is to get a good fare if you wait."

"Pete, my family has never had a reunion before. Some of my relatives haven't even seen her!" Mom's pleading with her eyes; they're all sparkly.

Dad just stares at her.

"Oh, go ahead, then," says Mom throwing her arms up. "Book her a flight to Colorado Springs. You know you will anyway."

"Mumma," Dad grabs Mom gently by the shoulders, "don't you see? This whole summer is up in the air. I don't know how I'll be feeling then. I don't know if I'll be up to driving that far. We might all have to miss the reunion. Let's at least give Leah something to look forward to, okay?"

"Leah," says Mary. "Come here, quick! The baby's moving!" Mary pulls up her shirt and holds my hand to her stomach. It's hard, like a basketball. I don't see how a tiny baby can make itself felt through that, but there it is.

"Whoa!" I pull my hand away quickly and watch the bumps of little knuckles or toes swipe across Mary's domed stomach. "That's so weird!"

Paul, Mom, and Gram take turns feeling Mary's moving belly. Dad just watches.

CHAPTER 5

Monday, June 23

When I asked Dad if he and mom could drop me off at the mall on their way to his appointment he acted like it was no problem. "I'm your chauffeur, aren't I?"

But now that I'm captive in his car, he's giving me a hard time. "An exercise fiend like you could've run to the mall."

"Pops, it's ten miles!" Not to mention it's almost all uphill on the busiest highway in northern Michigan.

"What about riding your bike?"

"I could have, I guess, but I thought since you were going out anyway I'd be able to hitch a ride."

"Hitch a ride? The hospital's all the way on the other side of town."

I sit back and shut up. No use arguing with him when he's like this.

We turn into the mall and Dad suddenly panics. "I don't know how we're going to work picking you up, Leah. You won't want to wait around outside for us, and I certainly don't want to have to come in and go on a wild goose chase looking for you!" He's so flustered his ears are turning red. "I don't know how long this appointment is going to last. It might take a while."

Mom puts her hand on Dad's forearm. "Let's say four o'clock, Pete. That'll give us all plenty of time. You don't mind, do you, Leah?"

No, I shake my head. Heavens, no.

"Okay, then," says Dad, calmer now. "We'll pick you up right here at four o'clock."

I hit Sports World first. I love the smell of this place, all that new leather and rubber.

I look at shoes, balls, soccer gear. Finger the satiny materials on a rack of shorts. They're tempting, hanging there in their rainbow of colors, but I don't let myself stop. I have plenty at home.

I drag myself out, drooling, and head over to the bookstore. I've got business there. That's the real reason I came to the mall.

I find tons of books on cancer: books on prevention, books on detection, books on treatments, inspirational books written by people who've beaten it, even a cookbook with recipes that call for ingredients that supposedly fight cancer.

My hopes soar as I read about the many alternative treatments to chemotherapy and radiation—special diets, exercise regimens, meditation, hypnosis.

One book says you can get cancer from being unhappy for a long time, that cancer is "the manifestation of a deep-rooted psychological ill, a long pent-up frustration, suppressed ambition, emotional trauma, unresolved personal conflicts, job stress, even guilt." It says that if you identify the source of your unhappiness and eliminate it, you can rid yourself of cancer.

I've always thought of my dad as a basically happy person, but this makes me wonder: why did he get cancer? Not because he can get ornery sometimes, I'm sure.

I finally decide on two books—an inspirational account of recovery and a book on self-healing. Twenty minutes left. I speed-walk the length of the mall to General Nutrition Center. I'm going to get Dad some of that weird stuff I read about in the nutrition and self-healing books.

It's almost four o'clock when I leave the mall, a bag of books in one hand, shark's cartilage and ginseng tea in the other.

Mom and Dad are strangely quiet. I can't see Mom's face from the backseat, but I can see the wad of Kleenex she's clutching in her lap. Her other hand is holding Dad's. Probably not the best time to show them my purchases.

"How did your appointment go?"

Dad shrugs. "It's pretty much what I thought. Slim chance that experimental treatments would do any good, and you're almost certain to suffer more than if you let the disease run its natural course."

"So you're not going to try them? You've made up your mind, just like that?"

"That's right."

I sigh real loud.

"Now don't be giving me that," Dad growls. "Medicine isn't the answer to everything. Miracles can happen."

"That's right," says Mom. "We're putting this in God's

hands."

Well, at least they haven't completely given up.

When we get home, I wait for Dad to open a beer and sit down.

"Pops? Can I show you some things I bought at the mall?" I hand him the books first.

"One Man's Story of Bravery and Victory," Dad reads aloud. "Cancer: A Guide to Natural Self-Healing." He sets them down on the coffee table. "Thanks."

"That's not all, Pops. I got you some other things that I read about in the self-healing book." I hand him the GNC bag. "Ginseng tea and shark's cartilage. They're supposed to—"

"Shark's cartilage! Weez, you shouldn't be wasting your money on this stuff. They're gimmicks. If they worked, everybody would be taking them. They'd be charging an arm and a leg for these bottles."

"They weren't cheap," I mumble.

"The stores wouldn't be able to keep them on the shelf."

"This was the last bottle."

"Oh, Weez, don't be so naïve."

The way Dad says naïve stabs me. I don't say anything, just turn away from him and run towards the back of the house, to Gram's room.

"I was only trying to help, Gram. I thought he'd be happy. What's wrong with him? Why won't he even try things? It can't hurt."

40

"Come here, sweetie." She grabs my hand and pulls me onto the arm of her chair. "If you really want to help your dad, let me show you something."

She reaches under her bed and pulls out her pile of prayer books. "See this here booklet? This is St. Theresa, the Little Flower." A sad, young waif of a woman stares up at me from the cover. She's holding a bunch of flowers and is dressed in a hooded robe. "You pray to her once a day for nine days. If your prayer's going to be answered, she'll send you a flower."

"Is that true, Gram? Does she really?"

"If she's going to answer your prayer, yes."

"Has it ever worked for you?"

"Yes, it has. Twice."

"How? What happened?"

"Well, I'd been praying to her to help me get my house sold, and on this particular night I was baby-sitting for a young couple on our street who couldn't afford to go out much. It was their anniversary, so I offered to baby-sit for free. When they came home, guess what they brought me. A rose. From off their table at the restaurant. The next day somebody made an offer on my house."

"And the other time?"

"I can't tell you what I was praying for that time because it's personal. But I went to this huge supermarket grand opening and as I was walking through the parking lot I saw this rose in the snow. Just lying there, so red in that white snow. I'll never forget it. I picked it up, and later my prayer was answered."

Hmm.

"So that's the novena to St. Theresa, the Little Flower," says Gram. "There are others. You can say the novena to St. Jude. He's one of my favorites—the Patron Saint of the Impossible. They're all right here in these booklets."

"What's a novena?"

"It's Latin for nine. A novena is a nine-day devotion."

"What's so special about nine?"

Gram raises her eyebrows and cocks her head. "It might have to do with the Trinity—three times three equals nine? Something like that. Or you can say the rosary. That's what I do, once a day."

"Leah!" Mom calls from the kitchen. "Clay's on the phone."

"You better go, sweetie. Your little boyfriend's waiting." She says it with a straight face, too, and I give her a dirty look.

CHAPTER 6

Tuesday, June 24

I haven't touched a ball since Saturday and I've got a club practice tomorrow, so Clay and I go to the field at East Bay Elementary. It's cool and shady with big maples all around, and the grass is that soft stuff with real fine blades. The field's not that big, but it's private. Hardly anybody comes here during the summer.

We start with juggling. Clay and I have this thing—we both have to juggle a hundred times in a row before we can go on to the rest of our workout. Usually I'm done before him, but today he's already in the eighties and I've just started over for the fourth time.

I don't know what's wrong. I've got no touch. The ball's all over the place. By the time I hit forty, Clay's down on the ground doing crunches.

I lose control and drop the ball again. "Dang it!"

Clay's been really patient, but now he says, "You're probably warmed up enough, Leah. That's the point of juggling, right? Why don't we go on to something else?"

"No, Clay. No! Do I ever rush you?" I bark at him, and I know it's unfair. I've never had to wait long for him. But he should know better than to say something like that when I'm pissed off.

Finally, finally, I finish.

Clay throws me a water bottle. "What do you want to do today?"

"If you could serve me some crosses, that would be great. I also want to work on my one-touch finishing. What about you?"

"I was hoping we could time each other on some cone work. I need to get quicker with the ball, or I'm going to be sitting the bench again this year."

"Okay. Let's do that first."

Clay sets up an obstacle course with the orange cones and dribbles through it to show me what we have to do. He makes it fun, putting in these little surprises where you stop and do ten pushups, places where you dribble backwards.

We take turns timing each other, trying to better our speed with each round. My legs are lead. Clay's put in this grueling part where we have to stop and jump sideways over the ball twenty times before we can go on.

"Come on, Weez, a little faster. Push it! Twenty seconds down. You can do it!"

I'm hopping over the ball like a slalom skier — a slalom skier about to wipe out. I've lost my count, my timing, the feeling in my quads. I step on the ball and it squirts away. My legs fly out from under me and I land hard on my tailbone.

"Come on, Leah, get up! You can still do it!"

"No, I can't," I say, still sitting.

"Yes, you can! Come on!" Clay's bent over his watch like a

bomb's going to blow if I don't make my time. "Dig deep, Weez!

"Would you just shut up? You should hear yourself!" I brush the grass and dirt from my aching bottom and walk off the field.

"I'm not sure what I did, but I'm sorry," says Clay, following me. "Are you okay?"

I just shake my head and keep walking. When I'm sure I'm not going to cry, I turn around.

"I should have known it was too good to be true. I mean, I didn't expect to get a shot at the national team until after my freshman year in college. I thought I'd have to prove myself more. Accept a scholarship from some national power and show my stuff against the big name players in women's college soccer."

I pace back and forth, looking down at my feet, not really talking to him, just getting it out.

"But, no. Everything goes my way. I go to ODP camp and I'm chosen for the regional team. Which means I get to go to Colorado Springs to compete for a spot on the U-18 National Team. The U-18 National Team. That's one step away from the full national team, the World Cup, the Olympics.

"So I come home, high as a kite, and find out my dad is dying. And not only is he dying, but he has three months to live. He tells me this in June. National camp is in August. Do you think I'm going to miss the final weeks of my dad's life? Do you think I even care about soccer anymore?"

I stop and look at Clay.

"Yes, I do, or you wouldn't be talking like this. It bothers you, Leah. It bothers you that all of your soccer plans—your dreams—are all screwed up."

Clay is always so honest. I like that about him. But I hate it when he thinks he knows the inner workings of my mind.

"You don't get it, Clay. Soccer's the least important thing in my world right now. I can't enjoy it anymore. I mean, how can I keep coming out here, running around and having fun, when my dad is dying?" I wipe my eyes. "It's not fair. Why does this have to happen?"

Now, I want to say; why does this have to happen now? Just when I get to where I've been aiming, just when I should be enjoying myself.

"You can't think like that, Leah."

"Yes, I can."

"Well, you shouldn't. You shouldn't let it ruin your whole life. Yes, it's sad. And, yes, it's unfair. But remember what Mr. Schleeter says: 'Life's not fair.'"

I almost smile. Mr. Schleeter was our trig teacher. He was really hard on me. I'd ace a test, get every single answer right, and he'd take off points just because I hadn't shown my work. I'd complain about how unfair it was and he would boom over me, "Life's not fair!" The class thought it was a riot.

"Leah, you can't let it keep you from enjoying soccer. Your dad wouldn't want you to give it up on his account. Besides, he really isn't even that sick yet. There's always the chance that he might not die. Have you thought of that?"

He's right; I can't give up. In fact, I should do this for Dad.

Play soccer, make the national team, maybe even go to Notre Dame. Wouldn't he love that?

From now on, I'm dedicating everything I do to him. Every workout, run, practice, game. You know — win one for the Gipper.

"Clay, you should be a psychologist. You're really good at it." I slap him on the back.

A fresh blotchy spot spreads slowly on each of his cheeks until his whole face is aflame. He breaks into an ear-to-ear smile and turns away from me.

"Let's get back to it," he says.

"Yeah, we better. I haven't done a thing since ODP camp."

Wednesday, June 25

Climbing into the car with Dad, I realize I'd better enjoy this ride down to practice. After all, who knows how many more times he'll be able to do it?

It's two hours to Midland. Twice a week, three summers in a row, Dad's been driving me there. Sure, I wanted to play on a good team, but I never dreamed he'd be willing to drive that far, and I never would have asked. It was his idea. He wanted me to have tough competition, and there isn't much of that in our part of the state. People probably think we're wacko traveling so far to play on a club team, but we're not the only ones doing it.

Dad's in his classic pose: right hand at twelve o'clock on the steering wheel, left elbow out the window, hand grabbing onto the roof of the car.

I keep stealing glances at him when he's not looking. I want to remember every little detail so I'll never forget. Like the way he picks his nose with the tip of his thumb. And the way he spits out the window. When I was little, I used to think it was really cool how he hacked it up and let it fly. Whtt! Straight as a bullet. No mess, no spray, no blob—just a blur whizzing out the window. I'd try to do it just like him.

The radio station Dad listens to cracks me up. WXTC. He thinks he's so cool, but little does he know, he's a decade behind. These are the same songs he used to hate when Paul was a teenager blasting them in his bedroom.

Dad looks at me through his photo grays. "What's so funny?"

I realize I'm smiling but I can't tell him why. I'll tell him a Polish joke I heard at camp instead. Dad loves Polish jokes. "What the hell," he always says. "I'm a Polack. I can laugh at myself." He says they're the only jokes you can tell nowadays and not be called prejudiced.

"What happened when the Polack went to change his snow tires?"

"I don't know."

"They melted."

Dad laughs. "What happened when the Polack blew his nose?"

"What?"

"His head collapsed."

It's so stupidly crude, so Dad, that I have to laugh.

48

Funny thing is, while I'm thinking about enjoying every second I have with him, he doesn't even seem to know he's sick. You can't tell anything's wrong with him. He looks good. He's acting totally normal. He doesn't seem to be in pain. In fact, he doesn't mention it at all.

So I decide not to go for the record with him when his hand steals over across the seat. That wouldn't be normal enough for today. Today we have to act like everything's okay. For as long as we can, we have to act that way.

Coach Kenney paces in front us, twirling his whistle. When everyone's quiet, he faces us, planting his feet wide, crossing his hands behind his back.

"Before we start," says Coach Kenney, "congratulations are in order. As some of you may know, Leah made the regional team last week." He starts a round of applause, and I'm blushing like crazy, all hot under the collar. "It just goes to show what dedication can do for you."

Then comes Coach Kenney's lecture on dedication. "If you want to be really good, just practicing here with the team is not enough. You've got to practice on your own, at home, alone.

"Leah," he says, turning to me, "aside from games and practices, how much time do you put into soccer?"

Oh, geez, why is he doing this to me? I am kind of proud of my self-discipline, but it's a private thing. The others are going to think I'm nuts.

I feel a circle of eyes turn in on me, so I put on blinders and focus on Coach Kenney.

"I don't know. Maybe two or three hours a day, when the weather's good. In the winter I run and lift and do footwork in the garage. Sometimes I go to the school gym."

"There you go," Coach Kenney says to the team, smiling like I'm his own creation. "The proof is in the pudding."

Everyone's looking at me.

"I'm not trying to beat you over the head with this," Coach Kenney says. "Not everybody can be a Leah Weiczynkowski or a Michael Jordan." All eyes turn from me now. Probably in disgust. "And not everybody wants to be. It takes a lot of sacrifice. Maybe for you it's not worth it. And that doesn't make you a bad person. I just want you to be realistic about what you want to get out of soccer, about what you're putting into it, and about the balance between the two."

Man, I love practice. I get so into the drills. I'm like a racehorse pawing at the ground as I wait my turn in line. Then I'm out of the gates like a shot. Zoom, zoom, zoom! I try to do things crisp and clean. Make a run. Collect the ball. Turn. Take the shot. We've done these drills a thousand times, but I'm always after perfection.

We scrimmage, my favorite part. I'm free, running and romping, seeing what new success each shot or pass might bring. Can I put this ball in the net? Will I get an assist on this cross? Can I take this girl and beat her one-on-one?

The game is constant motion, back and forth, side to side. It's like jazz—nothing fits a pattern—yet it all comes together so perfectly.

Coach Kenney's whistle blows, and we jog over to the side-lines for a water break. I pause and sneak a look over at Dad sitting in the jeep. A newspaper's spread across the windshield so I can't see his face, but he seems to be doing okay. Then the newspaper drops and Dad's staring right at me. I quickly turn my head, embarrassed somehow, and squirt a stream of water into my mouth.

CHAPTER 7

Friday, June 27

It's noon and Mom still hasn't turned on the stereo. This isn't like her. She always plays music, from the time she gets up until we either turn on the TV or go to bed.

It's like a morgue in this house lately. Nobody says much. Nobody hangs around in the kitchen after meals anymore. Gram hides in her room. Mom and Dad go for walks or take the boat out. Dad goes to the restaurant and Mom digs around in the garden. Right now they're down at the beach, sitting in lawn chairs and staring out at the water.

Someone knocks on the front door and I run to answer it, hoping it's Clay.

It's a woman, maybe thirty-five or forty, with black curly hair and the tiniest nose and mouth I've ever seen. She's carrying a large tote bag.

"Hi. I'm Heather from Grand Traverse Hospice."

"Hello."

"Are your parents home?"

"They're outside. Down at the beach. I'll get them."

Hospice?

It's obvious they've been expecting her. She invites me to

join them. "In hospice we like to involve the whole family," she says, so I sit on the couch between Mom and Dad.

"You have a daughter," she says. "Any other family members living in your household?"

"I'm sorry," says Mom, "This is Leah, our youngest. We have two older children, Mary and Paul. They live downstate."

"Mom," I whisper, "don't forget Gram."

"Oh, yes. And Pete's mother lives with us. Do you want me to get her?"

"No, I'll meet her another time. Do you have any relatives living in the area?"

"No. We're from Milwaukee. Our families are still there."

"Have you told them about Pete's condition?" It's pretty clear this is a dialogue between Mom and the nurse, but the nurse keeps sending Dad these checking glances.

"Yes, we have," answers Mom.

"Good. Do you work, Rita?"

"I do the books for the restaurant and help out whenever I'm needed there, but someone can always cover for me."

"Then you'll be able to stay home and care for Pete?"

"Oh, yes," Mom answers.

"Good. And is that how you make your living, Pete, in the restaurant business?"

"That's right. Pete's Place."

"Pete's Place!" Heather smiles and clucks her tongue. "Oh, for heaven's sake. I go there! Great soups."

Dad smiles. "I thought you looked familiar. By now, most everyone in the area looks familiar. You meet a lot of people in this business."

"I bet you do," says Heather. "Your restaurant's a busy place. I've heard it's one of the few places that doesn't struggle when the tourists leave."

Dad is beaming.

Heather clears her throat and softens her voice. "Even though you're still doing well, Pete, Dr. Ross wanted us to meet before, ah, before the time comes when you will need our services. He said you've decided against any kind of treatment, and that you've signed a living will and papers stating that you wish to die at home. Is that correct?"

A chill shoots up my spine.

Dad nods. "Yes."

"So, from now on, I'll be coming into your home to give you all of your medical care. Our goal is to make you as comfortable as possible, to do things the way you want them done.

I'm getting that same awful cold-at-the-core feeling I got when Dad first told me he had cancer.

"At first," Heather continues, "I'll make weekly visits. As your needs change, I'll come more frequently.

"Now, about your home. It's a single story, no stairs for Pete to climb, right?"

"That's right," says Mom.

"Would you mind giving me a tour so I can take a look at the layout? It's a beautiful home, by the way."

"What the hell," Dad whispers to me when they leave the room. "Is this woman a realtor or a nurse?"

"So you've got several options," Heather says to Mom when they return. "If you can let me know what you decide by next week, that'd be great. Then I can give them an idea of where to put things before they come."

"Who's them?" asks Dad. "What things?"

"Typically, we begin by bringing in a hospital bed, and—"

"A hospital bed?" Dad raises his voice. "What the hell! What's wrong with my own bed? I don't need a hospital bed!"

Heather continues as if uninterrupted, "—a walker, and a wheelchair. You won't need them right away, but they'll be here for you when you do."

Dad's red-in-the-face mad now. "I'm not going to waste money paying for equipment we don't need!"

"Don't worry. Insurance picks up everything."

Dad snorts. "So that's why insurance premiums are sky high!"

"Pops," I whisper, "settle down."

"Pete," says Mom.

Heather tilts her head and smiles at us, like, don't worry, I can handle this, I've been here before.

"Pete," she says, touching Dad's arm, "I know it's hard to come to terms with what's happening to you."

"Just say what you have to say," he grumbles.

"Are you a spiritual man, Pete?"

Dad looks at Mom. Mom who reads her Bible every night, Mom who begs him to go on retreats with her. Mom doesn't say anything. She lets Dad field this question on his own.

"What do you mean by spiritual?" asks Dad.

I don't know if Dad's spiritual or not. He goes to church on Sundays. He sings and recites all the prayers. He takes communion. He even goes to confession regularly. But I'm not sure if there's anything behind it.

Heather rephrases her question. "Are you religious? Do you have faith?"

"Well, yes, I'd say so. I go to church, went to parochial schools as a kid."

"Okay, then. Stop and think about this over the next couple of days: Are there any wrongs you want to right, any people you want to reconcile with? Anything at all you need to do to put yourself at peace? Because if there is, now's the time to do it. While you still can. While you're still relatively healthy."

Geez, lady, give us a break!

I can't stand this. I've got to get out of here.

Heather takes Dad's blood pressure and heart rate. She listens to his lungs, checks his reflexes, feels his lymph nodes. She asks him about his sleeping habits, his appetite, his pain. "On a scale of one to five, five being the most unbearable pain imaginable, how would you rate your pain?"

"I don't know," says Dad. "I wouldn't say it's ever been over a four."

I try to think how bad that must be—a four. Of all the injuries I've ever had, my sprained ankle was the worst. Would that have been a four? I don't think so. I can imagine lots worse: getting scalped, having a limb amputated, blowing out a knee. Maybe my ankle was a three, if that. Poor Dad.

Heather closes her notebook. "You're quite jaundiced, Pete, but other than that your vital signs look very good."

She hands him some pamphlets. "I'll leave these for you to look over. One explains our philosophy and the other talks about the physical and emotional stages you're likely to go through." She smiles and shakes each of our hands. "I'll be back next week," she says, "unless I hear from you before then."

"She seems pretty nice," Dad says after Heather leaves.

If I had dentures they'd fall out right out of my mouth.

"Very nice," says Mom.

"Nice?" I cough in disbelief. "The woman is an iceberg! Didn't you think she was rude? How could she have the nerve to—?"

"Leah," says Dad, "that's her job."

CHAPTER 8

Thursday, July 3

I'm all packed for the Fourth of July tournament in Peoria, but Dad's curled up in the fetal position on the couch. He's been that way all morning.

I think that hospice nurse put ideas into his head. Ever since she was here last Friday he's been acting really weird. On the way home from my club match last Saturday he started wincing and doubling over the steering wheel.

"Could you drive for me, Weez?" he finally asked. "I'm not feeling too well."

That was the day after Heather came and started all that talk about dying.

So I knew. I knew a few days ago he might not be able to drive me.

He hasn't said we're not going, though. All he's said is, "Let me rest for a while. I might feel better." But I have this feeling. It's already ten o'clock, and we have to leave by noon at the very latest.

"Weez?" Dad props himself up on one elbow. "I don't think I'm up to driving. But there's still time for your mom to get you down there to carpool with someone."

"No. If you're not going, I'm not going."

"Come on, Weez. The team needs you. Don't let them down." He forces a smile. "I'll still be here when you get back."

"Very funny, Dad, but no."

"Come on. I feel bad enough that I can't drive you. Don't make me feel guilty that I'm making you miss the tournament, too."

"Okay, if you really want me to."

Dad asks Mom to call the other club team parents. She nods, this mischievous look in her eye, and takes the cordless phone into the back hall.

I press my ear against the back hall door. "It'll be a spontaneous family reunion," I hear Mom say. "Pete will be so surprised."

She's on the phone all right, but not with club team parents. I'll be darned if she isn't calling Dad's brothers and inviting them all for the weekend.

I push open the door. "What are you doing, Mom? Two family reunions in one summer? Isn't that a bit much? How's everyone going to be able to get up here on such short notice?"

"Honey, this may be the last time Dad and his brothers can all get together and have a good time. Everybody understands that."

"Do I have to stay home for it?"

"You'll have to decide for yourself what's more important to you."

Gee, Mom has such a way with words. Now if I go I'll feel like dirt.

"But he wants me to go. You heard him."

"That because he doesn't know everybody's coming. And he wouldn't tell you not to go, anyway. He knows how much soccer means to you."

"What are you going to tell him about why you're not driving me down to Midland?"

"We'll tell him everyone left already. We were too late."

Friday, July 4th

"How's the soccer star?" Uncle Frank bellows. He gives me a big wet one right on the lips. Ugh. The uncles are such a smoochy bunch.

"Hey, Pele! Get over here and give your uncle a kiss." Uncle Keith is the worst. He has a beard, so his kisses are prickly as well as wet.

"Score any goals for me lately?" Uncle Al always says the same thing.

I wish they would quit mentioning soccer. All it does is reminds me of where I'm not.

I don't believe it. Less than twenty-four hours' notice, and everyone's here.

Gram's finally come out of her room and she's in heaven. She takes over. "Rita, now don't you go doing any cooking. We'll have food brought over from the restaurant."

Mom nods. She knows better than to challenge Gram when she's in her element. She smiles and winks at me. "See? Wasn't this a good idea?"

Whenever the uncles get together there's lots of beer drinking, lots of big, stinky cigars, lots of gambling, and lots of loud voices. They're large, meaty men with dark complexions and dark curly hair. You'd never know that they're Polish. They look more like a Mafia clan.

It's only in comparison to my uncles that I notice how thin and pale Dad is.

Nobody's brought up the subject, though. We're just sitting around the living room now, the uncles and me and the older cousins, watching a Tigers game. The women are outside on the deck, and the younger kids are playing down at the beach.

I yawn, for the hundredth time today. I'm just sitting here, staring at the TV, hardly talking to anyone. I can't get out of this funk. I know it's selfish, but I can't help it. I'm not supposed to be here.

Right about now we'd be finishing our second round match. It's been itching at me all day, knowing everybody's out there improving while I'm sitting here going soft. The place is probably swarming with college coaches, too. Someone from North Carolina might even be there.

The little ones come inside and suddenly the living room's crowded and noisy. "When are we going to eat?" they all ask at once.

"Go ask Grandma," I tell them.

Hard as we try to send them away, they keep coming back. There aren't enough seats, and people are sitting against walls or other people's knees. Dad's lying on the floor with a couch pillow under his head. I'm straddling one arm of Uncle Frank's recliner; my favorite cousin Cheryl—she's seventeen, too—is perched on the other.

Jared—he's nine—comes up behind me and stands so close he's breathing down my neck. "Is your dad going to die?" he whispers.

"No," I say quietly. "He hasn't even had to start treatments yet."

"Good, because my dad's afraid he's going die."

"That's silly," I say, and mess up his hair.

"How is your dad doing?" Cheryl asks.

"See for yourself."

The little kids are jumping on him like he's a trampoline, begging him for airplane rides. He's tossing them around, wrestling them down, tickling them. Just like he always does. He hardly looks like a dying man to me.

Cheryl screws up her mouth. "But what about his—?"

"I don't know anything more than you, Cheryl. Really. It's all inside. You can't tell how bad it is except by what he lets on."

I don't think the little kids even know that Dad's sick.

Gram ordered Dad's favorite meal from the restaurant—lamb chops, baked potatoes, corn-on-the-cob —but he doesn't eat much. As soon as the tables are cleared, the adults set up for a card game. It's a nighttime ritual at family gatherings. They play Sheep's Head, dime a chip.

They're quite an event, these card games. Lots of whooping it up and good-natured ribbing. The uncles slip the little kids dimes to fetch them beers. I used to love that.

Mom is famous for falling asleep while they're playing. She sits there nodding, glasses sliding down her nose, this silly grin on her face. The person next to her has to nudge her when it's her turn. She never knows what's been played, and it drives Dad crazy.

Gram divides the chips and passes them out. She shuffles the deck, gives her thumb a quick lick, and expertly flips the cards around the table.

I feel better now that it's nighttime and the games are over in Peoria.

Mom's right. This just might be the last time we can all get together like this. I sit back and pan around the table, soaking it all in.

Aunt Evie's cackle.

The haze of smoke hanging over the table.

The prune-ended stubs of cigars gathering in ashtrays.

Green and brown and clear beer bottles crowding the table. Pabst, Old Milwaukee, Miller, Coors, Bud, Heineken. Everyone has a favorite brand.

Uncle Al accusing Uncle Frank of cheating: "I can tell by that look on your face, Frank. I don't trust you any further than I can throw you!"

Aunt Sherry with a book in her lap, reading between turns.

Little kids sitting on laps, building towers out of the piles of coins.

Mom's music swirling and floating in the background.

Ever since I can remember it's been this way. Except — my

camera freezes—except tonight Dad's the one dozing and Mom's wide awake.

"Hey, Petey," says Uncle Joey, "wake up. It's your turn."

Dad straightens up and shakes his head.

"You're worse than your wife!" teases Uncle Joey.

"What the hell! I'm sick!" Dad barks at Uncle Joey. "What do you expect?"

Nobody can believe it. Dad can always take a joke.

Gram throws her cards in and stands up. "Time for fireworks," she announces. "It's plenty dark enough now."

The uncles build a bonfire on the beach, and everyone pulls up a chair or sits in the sand. Dad and Uncle Frank stand on the dock and launch the fireworks over the bay. Dad unwraps them and places them into position. Uncle Frank leans over, sucking hard on his cigar, and lights them with its glowing orange end.

We're not the only ones. Bonfires dot the peninsula shoreline, and the sky fizzles with crisscrossing fireworks. You can hear muted clapping and oohs and aahs coming from all along the bay.

After the grand finale, Gram gets up from her chair. "We'd better call it a night," she says. And her little automatons, all grown up into thick-waisted men, promptly obey her. "Aw, Ma," they gripe. One by one they line up and give her a kiss. Even Dad. I haven't seen him kiss Gram in a long time. She swats him gently on the bottom. "You rest well tonight, Petey."

As everyone's settling in for the night, I steal out for a run.

No one will even notice I'm gone.

Saturday, July 5th

This has been the slowest morning ever. It's pure torture knowing my team is up and playing again in Peoria.

Ten forty-five and Gram and her kitchen crew are still taking orders. It's like we've been eating breakfast all morning, intentionally dragging it out so that when Dad wakes up he won't realize how late it is.

Finally, we just start clearing the breakfast stuff away, and it's then that I hear my uncles and aunts whispering to each other.

"He's up. I saw Rita go into the bedroom with a tray."

Dad makes his first appearance round about lunchtime. He's in his blue bathrobe, carrying a cup of coffee as he comes down the hall.

"Morning, morning," he says, nodding to everyone like he's the mayor going through town.

"Glad to see you got a good night's sleep, Petey," says Gram. Dad raises his eyebrows. Right.

It's obvious he's not feeling well. His volume is down several notches, his movements slow and labored. He doesn't bother to get dressed, just sits down and turns on the TV and starts watching some golf tournament.

"I really want to see who wins this one," he says. His way of announcing that this is what he's going to do all day?

And so our day-in-limbo continues, the hushed voices of the announcers practically lulling me asleep. It's beautiful outside, and we'd all like to do something other than watch TV, I'm sure, but no one dares take the party elsewhere. The uncles hang around Dad.

Mom's worried, I can tell. "All this company is too much for him, don't you think? Oh, well. They go home tomorrow."

I try my best, but I'm afraid I'm not much fun.

They're still playing in Peoria.

Sunday, July 6

"Take it easy, Pete." Uncle Al shakes Dad's hand and whacks him on the back.

"Take it easy, Al."

"Take care of yourself, Petey." That's about as sentimental as anyone gets. The Weiczynkowskis are a pretty tough bunch.

I wave, and my cousins hang out the windows waving back. Mom and my aunts exchange blown kisses. I'm relieved it's nothing emotional, though, the pulling out of the Weiczynkowski caravan.

We're all about ready to collapse.

"I think I'll rest for a while," says Gram. "I haven't said my rosary all weekend." She turns and shuffles down the hall, back to how she was before her boys came.

Dad drags himself up out of his chair. "I better go out and take the tents down and bring in the sleeping bags. It's supposed to rain tonight."

Mom and I start to clean up, but we aren't putting a dent in the mess. All those beer bottles, dirty ashtrays, dishes everywhere. Ugh.

"Let's finish what we're doing so it doesn't stink in here," says Mom, "and then let's just lie in the sun all afternoon."

Mom and I are walking down the woodchip path to the beach, our arms laden with magazines, pillows, towels, and snacks. Suddenly Mom drops her load. Just lets it fall.

I look down at the mess in the woodchips — pretzels everywhere, the National Geographic splayed open with maps falling out, towels that will be full of slivers — and then I look at Mom. She's frozen in place, eyes huge with fear.

I follow her eyes through the tall, lacy ferns. An animal? A snake?

I don't see anything.

"Pete! Oh, Pete!" Mom gasps, "Are you all right?"

She flails through the ferns to the clearing where the tents lie collapsed on the ground.

There he is, slumped up against a tree trunk, his cheek pressed against the rough bark.

"Pete, are you all right?" Mom asks again.

Dad nods, then shakes his head, his eyes pressed tightly shut.

"What happened? What's wrong?"

He holds up his hand — not now, I can't. He's trembling.

I run over beside Mom. My heart's about to beat right out of my chest.

"What do I do?" Mom whispers to me.

"Call an ambulance!" I shout.

"No, you heard Heather. From now on Dad's under

hospice's care."

I can't believe it. We should be rushing him to the hospital! I run up to the house, rattling the windows as I stomp across the deck.

I call the hospice number on the fridge. "I think my dad's having an attack. Pete. Pete Weiczynkowski. Please, send somebody right away!"

Gram comes scurrying down the hall. "What's wrong?"

"It's Dad, Gram. He fell down outside."

Gram closes her eyes and crosses herself. "Hail Mary, full of grace . . ."

CHAPTER 9

Mom and Gram and I carry Dad into the house and lay him on the couch. By the time Heather arrives, he seems to be over the worst of it, but he's so exhausted he can barely talk.

Heather pats his arm and takes the stethoscope out of her ears.

"What happened?" Mom asks.

"From what I can tell, it looks like he got hit with an intense bout of pain."

"Are you sure? He couldn't move. He couldn't talk."

"Pain can be a very debilitating thing. The first time it hits you with that kind of intensity it takes you totally by surprise."

Dad jerks into total alertness. "You mean it's going to happen again?"

Heather touches his arm. "In all honesty, Pete, probably. And the frequency usually increases as well. But there are things we can do."

"Like what?"

"I'm going to start you on some things to help you control the pain."

"You mean painkillers."

"Yes, Pete." Heather speaks so soothingly. "For pain like you experienced today I'm giving you something called

Roxanol. It's a fluid. You mix it in a small amount of orange juice as soon as you feel the pain coming on and drink it down."

"Is it addictive?" asks Dad.

"Yes. It's very strong. And these pills," she says, handing him a bottle, "are for lesser, more general pain. I want you to take one first thing in the morning and one in the evening. They're timed-release so you always have some in your system. Between the two you should be able to manage your pain pretty well."

She also gives him some sleeping pills and anti-anxiety medication.

All I can think is, thank God we didn't go to Peoria.

Monday, July 7th

It's a hazy day and the lake is like glass.

"Let's just drift," Clay says, cutting the motor. Then he starts to laugh.

"What?"

"Nothing." But he snickers again, and the way he does it, I can tell he's laughing at me.

"What?"

"It looks like you're wearing your bathing suit on top of a white uniform."

I look down. Except for my forearms and the small section of my legs between where the top of my shin guards and the bottom of my shorts go, I'm white as a ghost. So I never got rid of my soccer tan from the week at ODP. Ha, ha. I haven't exactly been in the mood to hang out at the beach lately.

It makes me really mad, Clay looking at me and laughing. I cross my arms over my chest and give him a good looking-over, but I can't find anything to make fun of. Nothing. No zits, no buck teeth, no braces, no wax in his ears, no weird-shaped toes. He's not skinny or fat. He's perfect—a perfectly bronzed beach boy in mirrored Ray Bans and a stylish pair of swim trunks.

I'm not into teasing right now, anyway. I'd rather tell him about Dad.

I lean back, slouching down in the soft vinyl seat of Clay's boat. "My Dad's been getting these pains. It's terrible. You can tell when it hits him because he closes his eyes and grips something so hard his fingers go white. Then the trembling starts." A lump is rising in my throat.

"It must be really hard to watch," says Clay.

"It's awful. I mean, I've been in a lot of pain before, but nothing like this. I can't even imagine it. He can't put an ice bag on it and numb it, can't get off of it and rest it. Changing positions doesn't help. He just has to give in to this invisible beating. The nurse came and gave him this painkiller called Roxanol. It's straight morphine. But it either takes a while to kick in or his last dose is wearing off, and he absolutely refuses to take it again before he's supposed to. He's afraid of getting addicted to it."

"Afraid of getting addicted? Who cares!" says Clay. "I mean, if he's going to die—"

"I know."

I'm not going to cry today. I'm not. Not in front of Clay.

"Hey, you better put on some sunscreen or you're going to burn your lily white uniform." Clay reaches for the sunscreen. "Turn around. I'll put some on your back."

"I can get it," I say, taking the bottle from him.

He's watches me, smiling the whole time. "You missed a spot."

"Whatever. Here," I say and throw the bottle at him. "Go ahead if you're so worried about it."

Clay puts on lotion like he does everything else—meticulously. When he gets near my straps, he paints it on with one fingertip. How can hands feel so much like ice on a hot summer day?

He wipes his hands on his chest and reaches in the cooler for Cokes. I usually try to stay away from caffeine, but I take one anyway.

"I thought your family had a big reunion this weekend."

"We did."

"How was it?"

I scrunch my nose. "It's hard to have a good time when you're trying so hard. And I had to miss my tournament in Peoria."

"That's too bad. Speaking of soccer, have you gotten any more calls from college coaches?"

"Oh, geez!" I knock myself on the forehead. "I was supposed to call that coach from Notre Dame back!"

"Leah, I can't believe you. Don't blow this."

"I know, but what am I supposed to tell them when they

want to set up an official visit?"

"Be honest."

"I can't."

"Leah, if your dad knew his secret was screwing up your future, he'd want you to tell them. Besides, what are the chances those coaches would know anyone around here? Pretty slim."

"You're right. The reason he doesn't want anyone to know is because he's afraid they'll treat him differently. But I promised him I wouldn't say anything. I don't want to lie, Clay."

"Leah, people are going to find out. I mean, how many days of work has he missed? And what did you tell your club coach about missing the tournament in Peoria?"

"I told him Dad got the flu on the way down and we had to turn around."

"See? You're already telling lies."

I laugh, and Coke sprays out my nose. To make matters worse a burp's rising in my throat—a big one. I already have Coke streaming out of my nostrils, so what the heck. It's only Clay.

I let it rip.

"Leah!"

"Oh, don't get all stuffy on me. You know you want to, too."

Clay burps a weak little burp and smiles an even weaker smile. It's against his nature to be crude. His family is very proper. I was going somewhere with them once and somebody farted. It stunk up their whole car. Nobody laughed or said anything. They didn't even roll down the windows.

Mom and Heather are sitting at the dining room table when I get home.

"What's going on?"

"Shh!" Mom shoots a finger to her lips and nods at the couch. Dad's lying there sleeping, white as a ghost and covered in sweat.

"Sorry," I whisper.

"Another bout of pain," says Heather.

Mom flashes her bloodshot eyes at me and smiles. "I called Heather because your dad's changed his mind. He's going to try the experimental treatments."

I pump my fists in the air. "I knew it! I knew he'd come around!"

CHAPTER 10

Tuesday, July 8

I feel like Clay's my shrink. I'm always unloading on him, crying on his shoulder, or whispering into the telephone like this.

"Dad's finally decided to try the experimental treatments. He says nothing could be worse than the pain he's feeling now." I deepen my voice to sound like Dad's. "'I'll never last to see Mary's baby at this rate, much less see Leah make that team.' He still wants me to go to national camp."

"Do you have your ticket to Colorado Springs?"

"Yes, but that doesn't mean I'm going. I can't very well go if he's on his deathbed. Besides, I haven't played in so long."

"Oh, come on; it's been less than a week."

"It feels longer."

"You'll be fine. And that's really great about your dad."

"Isn't it? I feel like there's hope now."

"Have you talked to the college coaches yet?"

"Not yet."

"Leah." The way his voice dips I can tell he's really disappointed. "You've got to be kidding."

"Quit bugging me about it, Clay. It's my problem, not yours."

"Do you know how many people would give their right arm for a chance like this? I'm telling you, if I had even one half your talent—"

If he had half my talent! Poor baby. He's got it so tough. The last thing I need right now is his guilt trip. Does he think I like this? Does he think I don't want to play college soccer?

"What are you talking about, Clay? Or should I call you Clayton Thayer McGowen the third. Your parents have so much money you don't have to worry about college. You want to go to Harvard. Ivy League schools don't even give out athletic scholarships, so don't give me this If–I–had–half–your–talent crap."

All of a sudden I'm yelling at him. I'm really flipping out.

"You're a filthy rich brat and you and your whole life are perfect. I don't know why I thought I could ask you for advice; you don't know anything about problems. And I am not living your dream either, so go find your own!"

I hang up on him, and boy, does it feel good.

CHAPTER 11

Thursday, July 10

Paul came up last night so he can help Mom drive Dad down to Ann Arbor for the procedure today. He's getting Dad's breakfast while Mom and I are in their bedroom packing for the trip.

"It's not supposed to take very long or be very complicated," says Mom. "Dad will be in and out. We can bring him back home in a couple days."

I hand her Dad's dopp kit. "What exactly are they going to do to him?"

"They're going to put a tiny pump inside him, right where the cancer is. It will administer drugs to the area, drip after drip, all day long. That's how they're going to do chemotherapy. They think it'll be more effective than having him take it orally or intravenously, because they'll be able to send it directly to the area. That way it'll be more concentrated, and the side effects won't be as bad as they are when the drugs circulate throughout the entire body."

I help Mom carry stuff out and arrange the backseat for Dad with quilts and pillows.

When I get out, he's standing there hunched over, one arm leaning against the car. "Thanks for making my bed, Weez."

His voice sounds forced, like he's holding his breath. "We'll be back in a couple days. Be good to your Grandma."

Where is Gram? I look around. Paul makes a quick "over there" with his eyes towards the house. There she is, peering out the bathroom window. She ducks out of the way when she sees me looking at her. Poor Gram. I wish I hadn't looked.

I kiss Dad as Paul lends him an elbow and helps him into the car. Dad ducks in slowly. Even in the plush back seat he doesn't look comfortable.

After Paul closes Dad's door, everyone has glassy eyes. Mom and Paul don't say goodbye, just look at me and try to smile.

As they drive away, I look long and hard at Dad's head through the back window. I have a terrible feeling this might be the last time I see him.

It's just Gram and me. Alone and waiting. A whole weekend alone together. I wish I hadn't gotten in that fight with Clay, but I want him to know how mad he makes me.

This is the perfect time to call Coach McNall and the other coaches, with Mom and Dad gone now and Gram in the bathroom. I've got to get this monkey off my back.

My heart is racing as I punch in the phone number. What a chicken.

"Notre Dame Soccer." It's Coach McNall.

"Hi. This is Leah Weiczynkowski."

"Leah! Good to hear from you."

"I'm sorry I didn't get back to you sooner about planning an

78

official visit, but my dad is really sick, and I can't commit to a date right now. I just wanted to tell you that."

There. It's out.

"I'm sorry to hear that. Is he going to be okay?"

"He's got cancer."

"Oh, I'm so sorry."

"I would've told you sooner, but he didn't want anyone to know. He still doesn't, but I thought it'd be okay to tell you."

"Thanks for telling me, Leah. I was a little concerned when you hadn't called back. We're very interested in you, you know. Don't worry about the official visit. It can wait. And again, I'm so sorry about your dad."

When I hang up, that awful weight is gone.

Wouldn't Clay be proud of me?

Friday, July 11

This hulking man is ringing our doorbell. Two skinny younger guys are coming up behind him carrying some huge metal contraption.

"American Cancer Society," says the big guy. "We've delivering the equipment you ordered. Where do you want the bed?" He hoists up his pants.

"Um, I don't know. Let me go ask."

Gram's at the kitchen sink rinsing our breakfast dishes.

"Gram, some guys are here from the American Cancer Society. They're delivering a hospital bed, and they want to know where to put it. What should I tell them?"

She holds up her hand, I'll take care of it, and marches to the front door.

"There must be some mistake," Gram says to the man. "We don't need that thing. You can take it back."

"Hey, all I know is somebody put in an order to this address and it's my job to deliver it."

"Well, no one here ordered it."

"Maybe not, ma'am, but hospice did. Is someone here under hospice care?"

"Yes, but he's fine. We don't need it."

"If I could use your phone, ma'am, I'll call the main office and see if there's been some mistake."

Gram leads him in to the phone while I stay at the door, guarding it, so these two guys can't sneak the bed in behind our backs.

"They said hospice requested it," I hear the big man say to Gram. "It could be weeks before another bed becomes available, and this is a good one. I'd take it if I were you."

Gram hesitates. "Fine. But where on earth are we going to put it?"

"How about Paul's old room?" I say.

"That's a good idea. It's just a sewing room now."

The guys bring in the bed and clang around setting it up. They carry in a mattress, a walker, and a wheelchair. The big guy gives Gram some papers to sign, and then they're gone.

After they leave I take the wheelchair and the walker out to the garage, fold them up, and throw a boat tarp over them. But there's nothing we can do with the bed. We can't even budge it.

Gram closes the door to Paul's room, and we don't say another word about it.

Saturday, July 12

When I wake up, everything washes over me at once. I remember Mom and Dad are gone, and why. I remember that I haven't spoken to Clay since I hung up on him four days ago. I don't even want to get out of bed.

Well, it looks like the highlight of my day will be walking up to get the mail. Lately I've been getting letters from colleges coaches all over the country.

I wait until it's ten-thirty and I know the mail's there, and then I mosey up to the end of the drive.

It's kind of fun getting the mail: Let's see, who wants me today? I stand in front of the mailbox and rub my hands together to stir up some luck.

So much junk. Catalogs, magazines, bills. And seven letters for me! One from Texas, one from Penn State, one from Clay, one from SMU, one from Drake—

One from Clay? I tear it open.

> Dear Leah,
>
> I'm not sure what happened, but I'm sorry about our phone call the other day. I know you're going through a lot right now, and you're right, I should mind my own business and quit getting on your case about how you're handling the phone calls from college coaches.

Let me know when you feel like doing something. I'm here.

Love, Clay

P.S. I can't help it that I was born into the family I was any more than you can help it that your Dad is sick.

Love? What does he mean by Love? He can't love me. We're best friends. I would never write love in a letter to him. I might sign it your friend, but never love. He knows how I feel about that. He wouldn't write that just to bug me, either, especially not when he's trying to apologize. And he wouldn't throw it in there casually, like, Luv ya! That's not his style. No, if he wrote it, he meant it.

This ruins everything. How can I do anything with him anymore, knowing how he feels? I wouldn't know how to act.

So all this time he's been pretending, buttering me up, waiting, hoping I'll come around, or grow up, or whatever. Mom and Gram were right.

I guess I should have seen it. How he was looking at me the other day on his boat. How he tried to put his arm around me the night I told him about Dad. He must really like me, too, if I haven't driven him off with my burping and sweaty grossness. Not exactly sexy stuff.

I shove the letter back into the envelope; I don't want to think about it.

CHAPTER 12

Sunday, July 13

You'd think the President's coming to visit, the way Gram's acting. We even skipped church today. She wants everything to be perfect. We've cleaned every square inch of the house, and Gram's cooking up a storm.

We hear the car pull in and run to the door.

Paul helps Dad out of the car, and I wait for him to rise to his full height, but he never does. He's hunched over like an old man. Paul gives Dad an elbow and guides him up the walkway. Dad's leaning heavily on Paul, grimacing.

I must look worried because Mom comes in ahead of them and whispers to us. "Don't worry. He's fine, just sore from the incision."

"Hey, Pops, welcome home!"

"Hey, Weez," he says flatly. "Did you hold down the fort for us while we were gone?"

I smile, glad to hear his lines are still the same even if his delivery is off. Because, boy, is it off. His voice is weak and airy. He looks a lot thinner, too. I can see the hollows in his cheekbones. Maybe it's a good thing the American Cancer Society brought that stuff. It looks like he's going to be needing it. He could use that walker right now, that's for sure.

Friday, July 18

I'm in the front yard juggling and I've got this amazing string going—I could break my record right here and now—when I hear a car coming down the drive. Shoot! I don't need any interruptions now.

It's Heather.

"Well, I'm glad to see you out here playing," says Heather. "Things must not be too bad, then."

I lose my rhythm and the ball squirts into a pine tree. "What do you mean?"

"You don't know? Your mom called the office and asked for me. They contacted me right away, said she sounded really upset."

Huh? I wonder what's going on inside. Besides the usual, that is—the chemo making Dad sick and cranky.

Mom's sitting on the edge of the couch by Dad, holding a wastebasket. He looks like a wax statue, lying there so still and white.

"It's been a week, Heather," says Mom, "and the chemotherapy isn't doing any good. He's tired. He's sick. He's losing weight. And look at his legs!"

Dad's legs are puffy, almost lumpy in places, and the skin looks soft and spongy. But when Heather touches them, her fingers don't sink in at all.

"I'm not sure what this is," says Heather, "but chemotherapy, as you know, can be very hard on the body."

"I thought that was supposed to be the advantage of the pump—to lessen the side effects."

"It is, in theory, but remember, this treatment is experimental. There's still a lot we don't know. This treatment doesn't come with any promises, Rita. Only hope."

"I know all that, but I can't stand to see him like this. I just can't bear it anymore." Mom's lips go tight and she shakes her head.

Heather turns her sweet china doll face to Mom. "It's hard, I know. But let's give it a little more time."

Mom's chin is quivering so I go over and hug her. She buries her face in my sweaty T-shirt and I can feel her whole body jiggling.

Sunday, July 20

We file into the pew, Mom and Gram and me. None of us sits in Dad's spot, the end seat by the aisle. We leave it empty.

Dad's legs are still swollen and they get worse if he's on them too long. Heather says he's supposed to stay off them and keep his feet up.

I wonder how Dad feels having to be baby-sat. He's at home with a young nurse named Jennifer who comes to spell us for a few hours. Our new priest, Father Pat, is coming to give him communion later.

I really like Father Pat. I understand what he's saying more than I did our old priest. I just couldn't get past all his thees, thous, and almighties.

Not only do I pay more attention in church now, but I also mean what I say instead of mumbling along with everyone else like I used to. It's amazing how fitting everything is. Funny I never noticed it all before.

We pray for the sick, have special times for our silent intentions—I pray for Dad, for North Carolina to call, that I'll get to go to Colorado.

Father Pat's sermon today is about faith. The Bible says that if you have faith the size of a mustard seed, nothing is impossible. Even with this small amount, you can move mountains. I like that.

Maybe Gram is onto something

But it's confusing, too. A few Sundays ago the homily was about how God works in mysterious ways. How we have to accept His will, no matter what. And even though we may not like what he's doing, we have to trust that it is for the best. We just can't see it. After that Sunday, I was ready to let Dad die, to say, Okay, God, if that's how it has to be, just take it easy on him, please, and help me cope with it.

Some days it feels okay to give up like that. But inevitably the guilt settles in, like I must be weak to think that way.

All it takes is faith the size of a mustard seed. Don't I have that? Because if I had enough faith, I could make Dad get better, couldn't I?

When we get home, Heather's there with Jennifer. Dad's sitting at the dining room table, his arms crossed over his chest and his eyebrows furrowed into an X. Heather is just sitting down across from him.

"What's the problem, Pete? Jennifer called and said you

were being difficult."

Mom and I exchange sheepish glances.

"No more," says Dad. "I can't take it anymore. Get this thing out of me."

"We can't take it out," Heather says calmly. "We told you that going in. We can stop administering chemotherapy with it, but the pump has to stay. Whether we leave it non-functioning or use it to administer painkillers, it has to stay."

"No," snaps Dad. "You are not going to use it for that. I will keep taking the painkillers orally. It damn well could be the only control I have left."

"Okay, then. We leave it empty. No more chemo."

"That's right."

Empty. That's how I feel right now.

"What a waste of time that was," mutters Dad.

Mom and I walk Heather and Jennifer to the door and stand there in our church clothes watching them go.

"I should've known better," Dad says. "I did know better. Don't let this happen again, Mumma. Please. Those papers I signed. Help me stick to my guns from now on."

CHAPTER 13

Tuesday, July 22

I hate the thought of going to club practice in Midland without Dad, but national camp is only twelve days away. I've got to be ready.

Enzo's my driver now. "I like this getting off afternoons," he says. "Normally, I'd be chopping lettuce this time of day."

I can't tell if he's serious. Enzo always looks as if he enjoys prep cooking the way he shows off, flashing his knife about, slicing and dicing like they do at Japanese steak houses.

"Do you mind driving me, Enzo?"

"Oh, no. This is one of the more interesting assignments your dad has given me over the years. You know I love soccer."

I smile and pat Enzo on the knee.

We don't talk any more about Dad. I don't think Enzo likes to think about what might happen any more than I do.

Everybody knows about Dad now. Mom told some employees at the restaurant, and the news spread quickly. But it's a good thing. A relief. We don't have to pretend anymore; we don't have to constantly try to keep the house looking like everything's normal just in case someone stops by.

I brought the walker out of hiding and set it up in the back hall, but Dad won't touch it. He's still shuffling around on his own, all hunched over.

When I get home from Midland, Mom and I join Dad in the living room and eat dinner in front of the TV.

Dad's been so restless lately. He roams from chair to couch, couch to chair, from lying on the floor to standing to kneeling.

"I can't get comfortable," he says.

If we walk in on him while he's resting, he fumbles around and tries to get to his feet. Mom says he doesn't want us to think he's lazy.

When Mom and I go to bed, he's still pacing. He says he's not tired yet.

I wake up during the night to use the bathroom, and all the lights are still on in the living room.

"Dad?"

He's kneeling over the ottoman.

"What're you doing? It's the middle of the night."

"I can't sleep. I didn't want to keep your mother up with my tossing and turning."

In the morning he's still there, the TV's still on, and he's tangled up in an afghan on the couch. I think the living room is his home base now.

After my breakfast is digested, I work out by myself at the East Bay Elementary field for a couple hours. When I come back for lunch, Dad is still on the couch. I think I woke him, because he sits up, all disoriented, and struggles to his feet.

"Got to keep moving," he says. "Got to get my stamina back."

He roams slowly about the house, down the hall and back, between rooms, settling finally on the back porch in a lawn chair. I take my sandwich out there and sit with him. I've been practicing all morning and have had enough of the sun, but I figure he might like the company.

Dad seeks out warm, sunny places; he complains of being cold all the time lately. But the warmth only seems to add to his drowsiness. It isn't five minutes before his speech starts slurring and his head is nodding.

I finish my sandwich in silence, noticing the beads of sweat popping out on Dad's forehead and upper lip. I'm afraid he's going to get heatstroke.

I go find Mom, and we guide Dad carefully into the house. He heads zombie-like for his couch, and Mom redirects him into the sunroom, onto the daybed.

"Oh, come on, Mumma," Dad mumbles. "I like the couch. What's the matter with the living room?" When he tries to get up, she gently pushes his shoulders back down.

"No, Pete, you need a change of scenery."

She turns on the ceiling fan and opens all the windows. There's a lovely breeze.

"Why don't you let him be where he wants to be?" I whisper in her ear.

Mom pulls me into the kitchen. "Because it's time we set him up in one room. And the sunroom is the most pleasant room in the house."

"What do you mean set him up?'"

"Heather says that as it gets harder for him to move around, he'll probably want to eat and sleep and spend most of his time in the same room. She says we'll all end up spending a lot of time in that room, that towards the end the whole family will practically be living in that one room."

Towards the end. Another one of those hospice phrases I hate.

Saturday, July 26th

Enzo brings Jake and Sam from the restaurant and they move the hospital bed into the sunroom.

Dad's watching TV in the living room and he's pretending not to notice the parade of men going back and forth. He knows why they're here and he must not be too happy about it — why else wouldn't he at least be civil and say hello?

When they finish, Mom makes the bed in the yellow gingham sheets I used when I was little. She drapes a cotton throw over the outside rail and puts a bunch of pillows against the other, and it doesn't look too bad. It almost looks like a twin to the daybed on the other side of the room.

With Enzo and the guys sipping lemonades in the wicker chairs and the hospital bed looking like something out of Better Homes and Gardens, you'd never know this was a sick room.

Enzo finishes his drink and says, "Will that do it for you, Mrs. W.?"

"Yes, thank you, Enzo. Leah and I never could have done it

by ourselves."

"Okay, then. We'll say goodbye to the boss and be on our way."

Enzo raises his eyebrows like he knows they're taking a foolish chance, but they go into the living room anyway.

CHAPTER 14

Sunday, July 27

I tuck my chin into my chest and pump my arms, trying to motivate my legs. This is only the second sprint interval in the Fartlek, and already they won't cooperate. It's like I'm running through water, my legs are so heavy.

I leave the road and take a trail into the woods. Maybe if I get out of the sun some of my energy will return. It's cool and dark in here; all the sounds are soft and muffled. Sump, sump, sump, sump go the leaves underfoot. I'm a metronome. My body drones on, one foot in front of the other in the same plodding rhythm.

It used to feel like I was running toward something, being pulled almost. But now I just feel this drag. It takes so much more effort than it used to.

I never realized how much I depended on Clay to push me. I think that's part of my problem. I've never had to think about pacing before—I just followed Clay. He made it seem so easy. He made it fun.

It's going to take self-discipline, that's all. I'll have to forget about him and learn to push myself.

Longer stride, I tell myself. Light on your feet. Bound, don't plod.

My step quickens and the pendulum swings faster. The trail is leading me now. My breathing is regular now, deep and slow. I'm no longer conscious of the movement of my feet or of the pulse and sounds of the woods.

When I get back to the house I pay Matilda a visit.

A couple years ago, Dad let me paint a rectangle as big as a regulation-size goal on the backside of the garage. I painted this hulking goalie in the middle of it. That's Matilda.

I dance like a boxer between punches as I wait for the ball to rebound. Then BLAM! A shot with my left. BLAM! A shot to my right. BLAM! Left. BLAM! Right.

What am I doing? I'm not working on placing shots past Matilda; I'm pummeling her.

National camp is a week away, and I've lost my focus.

I sole trap the ball and run into the house. Into my room. Reaching between the mattress and box spring, I pull out Clay's letter.

On my way back out through the kitchen, I grab a bowl and some matches.

Back behind the garage, I sit down against the wall, the bowl between my legs. I tear the letter into fingernail-sized bits.

He loves me, he loves me not.

Oh, how I wish he loved me not.

The last piece ends on he loves me not, but I know better. I drop a lit match into the bowl of confetti and watch it curl and burn. In a brief moment of violence, the letter is gone.

"Leah?"

It's Mom, lugging a bag full of garbage. I wonder how long she's been watching. If she notices the bowl between my legs, she doesn't say anything.

"What's the matter, honey? You seem all out of sorts. Is it Dad?"

"Yeah." I can hardly say no; I know that's what should be bothering me most. "That's part of it."

"What else?" She drops the garbage bag and slides down next to me. It's funny to see Mom in a skirt sitting in the dirt, her knees drawn up all ladylike.

Do I tell her all of it? About Clay? The college stuff? Colorado Springs? No, not all of it.

"Mom, I really need to know—do I have to go to the family reunion, or can I go to Colorado?"

"I guess it has been a long time since we talked about it."

"It has, and I know Dad got me a ticket to Colorado, but . . ."

Mom's pushing pebbles around in the dirt, not saying anything.

"I don't know, Mom. I kind of need to have it clarified."

She raises her eyebrows and does this little ho-dee-ho thing with her head, like we're playing a guessing game.

I refuse to beg. She knows what I'm after.

"Leah, if you're looking for me to tell you, 'Yes, you can go,' I'm sorry. I can't do that. Not at this point."

"Great. I knew you'd say that. So I don't know any more now than I did before. Colorado's next weekend, Mom!"

"I know it is," she says, softening. "How about I break it

down three ways for you, okay? One, if Dad's feeling well enough to drive to Milwaukee for the reunion, then we'll all go, you included. Two, if he's not up to driving, but is still doing basically okay, then you can go to Colorado Springs. Three, if he's not doing well at all, you will, of course, want to stay home. Fair enough?"

"Lovely, just lovely. What about what Dad wants? Doesn't he get a say in this?

"Leah."

"What would you tell me if Dad stays about the same as he is right now?"

"I'd say go to Colorado."

So basically, then, I'm hoping for Dad to feel somewhat crappy. Nice daughter, huh?

CHAPTER 15

Tuesday, July 29

It started happening a couple days ago. Dad will be hobbling along and he'll get this funny look on his face and freeze. Then he looks down to see this big wet spot growing on his pants between his legs. Poor guy. Yesterday his friends took him to the golf course so he could ride around in the cart and watch them play. He wet his pants, and they had to bring him home.

Heather says the cancer has grown and it's pressing against the nerves that control the bladder. She says that's why his legs are swollen, too; his body fluids are being trapped there by the tumor pushing on the veins that go back up to the heart.

So now he has to wear Depends. He's completely humiliated. Refuses to leave the house. "Not with this diaper on," he says.

We're out on the deck and Dad's standing over a lounge chair, one foot up, elbows resting on the knee. His eyes close and his head bobs. When the supporting knee begins to buckle, I say, "Dad, why don't you sit down? You're falling asleep."

Dad startles and grumbles, "I'm alright. Don't worry about me! I'm not asleep. I know what I'm doing."

He's irritated with me, so the next time the knee starts to

give way, I keep quiet I watch him teeter and bob, wondering if I can catch him if he falls.

And that's when he topples. I lunge, but I'm too far away to catch him, and he goes down hard on the wooden deck.

"Dad! Are you all right?"

"Yeah. I'm okay." He's slow in getting up, but he laughs and brushes himself off. "Boy, I went ass over teakettle there, didn't I?"

I'm on the back porch with Dad, keeping an eye on him again, making sure he doesn't fall asleep and topple over. After he fell this morning, I'm not taking any chances.

We're catching the last of the sun while Mom gets dinner. I'm sitting on the porch steps beneath him, pretending to be reading my Soccer America. Dad's standing over a lawn chair again. I don't know why he doesn't sit down and give his poor legs a break. Maybe sitting is uncomfortable. I don't know.

All I know is my feet are resting on the cement sidewalk that runs between the house and the garage, and that's where Dad will fall if he goes ass over teakettle again.

Out the corner of my eye I keep watch over just how relaxed he's getting. His head droops and bobs, his fingers twitch, and he mumbles, dreaming aloud. When his supporting knee begins to buckle, I quickly try to strike up conversation.

"Can you believe it, Dad? It says here that for the next Olympics—"

"What?" Dad flinches and jerks upright. "What?" His eyes go from scared and darting to focusing sharply on me. I'm being a pain, I know, and I'm not fooling him either.

He bites my head off. "You don't have to sit here and watch over me! I'm a big boy. I can take care of myself. Go do something." He shoos me away. I'm ten years old again, but my sense of duty is greater than my embarrassment, and I'm not going anywhere.

"Dad, I don't want you to fall off the porch and crack your head open. That's the last thing you need right now."

"Maybe that's exactly what I need," Dad snaps. "A nice solid blow to the head that'll do me in for good." He's so bitter it makes my nose prickle.

"Weez," he says, voice softening, "I don't need a baby-sitter. I'll be all right. You're a kid; you should be out there doing kid things, not hanging around here all day. Go run around. Go jump in the lake. Go do something for me, would you?"

I nod, choking up. "But I don't want you to get hurt."

I want to be strong and not cry. I want to be his tough Weez, but I can't. I lay my head down on my Soccer America, hiding my face with my arms. As I'm lying there, silently drenching the pages in tears and wishing Dad would hug me or put his hand on my head — anything — I hear something. Something as soft but as definite as snowflakes falling. I lift my eyes to the sound. It's tears. Tears splashing down onto the deck, the dry, sun-baked boards soaking them up as fast as they fall.

And suddenly it dawns on me; there's someone here who's hurting more than I am, someone big and grown up.

I look up at Dad. He's taken his glasses off and is swiping at his eyes with the back of his wrist. His eyes are pressed shut, but these fat droplets keep squeezing out from between his eyelids. They roll a ways down his cheek before they spill off or get brushed away.

I'm studying him, his head hanging, when his watery eyes blink open. He stares at me through a swell of tears and the pinkish-yellow of bloodshot, jaundiced eyes as if acknowledging his helplessness, as if accepting my pity. No denying anything now. We are at a moment of truth.

He opens his mouth, and I'm surprised at how in control he is.

"Look at me, Weez. I'm useless."

No, you're not, I want to say, but nothing will come out.

"This isn't living. Weez. This is no fun. Not for me, not for you. I'm tired of being a burden on everybody."

My heart is splintering.

"I've had enough. I want Jesus to come and take me to heaven. I'm not afraid of dying, Weez."

In the tenderest, calmest tone I've ever heard him use, Dad talks to me. Really talks to me.

It's not defeat in his voice; it's surrender. Voluntary, peaceful surrender.

"You know what Uncle Frank said to me? He said, 'Well, Pete, it looks like you get to be the first one to see Pa again.'" Dad smiles broadly, like he won the race.

I shake my head and smile.

"I'm going to heaven; what's so bad about that?" asks Dad.

I shrug.

"Don't worry about me. I'll be fine where I'm going."

"I know, but I'm going to miss you," I squeak.

Dad bows his head and starts crying.

We're quiet for a while, both sniffling.

But then Dad starts talking again. He tells me all his wishes, what he wants us to do for Mom, who gets what of his things.

It's the first time Dad has talked to me about any of this: dying, heaven, our life after he's gone. Mostly, I just listen. I have few words, only pity, sadness, closeness to him. I'm terrified to lose him, but I don't want to see him suffer like this either.

It's like Dad and I have knocked down this wall between us we hadn't even realized was there. As we move about the house, he keeps winking at me, smiling at me. I hear him go into the kitchen and tell Mom, "Mumma, Weez and I had a talk out there . . ." It seems to have made him happy.

I can cry around him now and I don't have to hide it. Tonight when we were outside on the deck waiting for dinner I broke down hard. Dad hobbled over and rubbed my shoulders. And he says he's useless.

It's hard to know what to pray for anymore. All along I've been praying for Dad to get better. I know there's still a chance for a miracle; there always is. But maybe that isn't what God has in mind for Dad. We all have to die, and Dad is ready to go.

He's accepted this as his time. Why shouldn't I?

CHAPTER 16

Friday, August 1

It doesn't look good. Colorado Springs, that is. Dad's not doing well. Personally, I think it's borderline, whether he's not doing well, or whether he's really not doing well, but I can just bet which way Mom will see it. The thing is, he might be going downhill, but he's not about to die. That much I can tell.

I ask Mom and she says, "Yes, I think a break would do you good."

I can't believe it.

"And it might do your dad some good as well. He needs something to be excited about. Go make that team for him."

I rush over and hug her, down low around the hips, picking her right up off the floor. "Thank you, Mommy Dearest! Oh, thank you!"

Mom's arms are flailing like I'm going to drop her.

"Leah, I'm too heavy!" Her bracelets are jangling and I can see the fillings in her top molars and her pink pearl fingernails waving through the air.

I'm loving every second of it.

Saturday, August 2

I'm on my last set of abs before bed, crunches with a twist, and I'm singing.

"I'm leaving . . . ugh . . . on a jet plane . . . ugh . . ." I've been singing that song all night, nonstop.

I lie down in bed and pull the hem of my T-shirt down all around, smoothing out the wrinkles under my back. I tuck the sheet up under my chin, folding it over my bedspread and wiggle my feet to make sure it isn't too tight down there. I've got to get a good night's sleep.

There's no moon tonight and I can't make out much of my Wall of Fame, just the outline of the frames against the wall. Where will I put this sucker once I get it home? Whatever it is—a medal, a plaque, a trophy, or a U-18 National Team photo—you can be sure of one thing: it'll be on that wall, front and center.

I say a prayer for Dad and one for luck in Colorado Springs, my fingers tracing the letters of my IWBTBWSPITW shirt. I've been wearing it to bed all week. It's a confidence booster, almost like—what do you call it? A subliminal message. I've been drilling it into my brain: I will be the best.

The letters are getting brittle. Last night the peeled-up B broke off. I obsessed about what to do—glue it or pin it or just throw it away—but then I fell asleep. I woke up this morning with the black curl of letter still in my hand.

Tonight I'll stay on my back and preserve this relic a little longer.

CHAPTER 17

Sunday, August 3

The airport shuttle van enters the Olympic Training Center and drops us off in front of a dorm. I take a deep breath, and I swear I can already feel the altitude.

A woman wearing US Soccer clothes herds us into the lobby. We wait in line for our room assignments, linens, ID meal cards, keys. I'm in room 309. Hot damn! Nine's my number.

I head for the elevators. All around me the lobby hums with activity. It's overwhelming, really. Hundreds of girls, dozens of coaches, soccer gear in every bright color. Girls rummaging through luggage. Keys and paperwork exchanging hands. Cell phones ringing.

I stand with a group of girls waiting for the elevator. While I'm checking them all out, they're just looking up at the numbers that light up as the elevator descends each floor. They seem so calm, like they've done this a hundred times.

Everyone looks so good. They're wearing T-shirts from the best all-star camps, beautiful silky uniforms only the premier club teams can afford. Shoes, shorts, shirts, socks, hats, bags — the whole ensemble Umbro or Adidas or Nike.

The elevator dings and its doors open. I step in, surrounded by a bunch of nose-in-the-air ODP prima donnas.

I feel so much better now that I have a game under my belt! Our North team just beat the East team three to one. I had a goal, so I'm pretty happy. We're cooling down now, getting ready to watch South play West in the last match of the night.

I lie in the grass and stretch my legs. Navy sky, field lights humming—everything's Technicolor. The grass is golf course green, the red is liquid blood red, the numbers on the jerseys and the lines on the fields stand out like they're made of reflective tape. Oh, it's good to be out on the field. A field is a field wherever you go. I don't feel so out of my element anymore.

Everyone's not as great as I thought they were going to be, either. I guess image isn't everything. Number eight, for instance. She might be fast, but her technique is awful. She dribbles with her head down. And number twenty-five? No left foot whatsoever. I haven't seen anyone out here yet who's the complete package.

After standing in line at the dorm pay phones for what seems like hours, I finally get to call home.

"Mom?"

"Leah! Dad and I were just wondering how you were doing."

"I'm doing great. It's incredible here. I'm so glad I didn't have to miss it."

"Me too."

I have to snicker.

"No, really. I'm happy for you. I wish we didn't have to miss

106

my family reunion, but you deserve this.

"Thanks, Mom. How's Dad doing? I felt kind of bad leaving."

"Oh, don't worry. He's actually relieved you went. He was afraid you might not go on his account. He so wanted you to have this chance."

"How's he doing? Can I talk to him?"

"It looks like he may be falling asleep, Leah."

"Okay, don't bother him then. Tell him I'll talk to him tomorrow."

Tuesday, August 5

My cleats against the sidewalk make me sound like a horse clopping along. I didn't want to take the time to change into my running shoes; I've got to beat everybody back to the dorm so I can be first in line at the pay phones.

I forgot to call home yesterday.

They keep us going from sunrise to sunset and then I fall dead asleep—the altitude wipes me out—so there's little time to think about home.

We're not playing as set teams anymore, no more North, South, East, West. They've been mixing us up and trying different match-ups, making cuts as they go. They don't post names, but the way they switch players around, it's obvious. My roommate was here last year, and she says if you're on the red or blue team they're really looking at you.

It's intense. Coaches sit on the sideline taking notes, jotting down a jersey number after someone does something good, crossing out others when they screw up. Everybody plays like her life is on the line.

Me, I played two full matches, so I'm dog-tired tonight. I can't believe I'm jogging now when I don't have to.

My hands are shaking as I punch in our number.

"Hi, Mom."

"Leah."

"How are you?"

"I'm fine."

She's not fine. She sounds mad.

"How's Dad?"

"He didn't have a good day today. Yesterday either."

Now I really feel guilty. "What's wrong?"

"I don't know. He's real groggy, slipping in and out of sleep all day. He's kind of unresponsive, doesn't even want to wake up to eat."

"Maybe he's catching up on all those weeks of not sleeping.

"Maybe."

"I had a great day today, Mom."

"You did?"

"I scored three goals."

"Wow, you must be in heaven."

"I am. Can I talk to Dad?

She puts the phone down, and I hear her say something to Dad. Then nothing. What's taking so long?

"Here he is," Mom's back on, whispering, " See if you can see what I mean."

"Hello?" This feeble voice comes over the line.

"Hi, Pops. Sorry I didn't call yesterday."

"Who didn't call yesterday?"

"Me, I—"

"Who is this?"

"Dad, it's Leah."

"Leanne? Leanne who?" His voice muffles. "Rita, do I know a Leanne?"

"No, Pops, it's Weez. Weez."

"Oh! Rita, it's Weez!" He laughs. "How are you, Weez? How's it going in Colorado?"

"Good, Pops. Real good. I'm doing well."

"That a girl. Say, did I tell you we climbed Pike's Peak in the Army?"

I laugh. "Only about a thousand times."

"We hiked up there with twenty-five pound packs on our backs. The air was so thin our noses wouldn't stop bleeding."

"Pops, Pops, I know."

"We camped in tents that night. It was so cold."

"I know, Pops, and all your water froze."

"Our water froze. My lips stuck to the canteen in the morning. But you could see for miles. Geez, it was beautiful up there."

"Pops, I remember all about Pikes Peak. How are you feeling?"

Nothing.

"Pops?"

Still nothing.

"Pops, are you there?"

"Weez?"

"What happened? Where'd you go?"

"Weez, I . . ."

It's like when you talk on the phone with someone overseas. There's that delay and you keep talking on top of each other.

"Go ahead, Pops." This is crazy, the two of us sputtering like this. "What were you going to say?"

"I don't remember," he says flatly.

"Here, Pete," I hear Mom say. "Say goodbye. You're getting tired."

"Bye, Weez. Give 'em hell, you hear me?"

"I will, Pops. Love you."

"Me, too."

Well, this is it—the biggest game of my life. And it's my favorite kind of day. Overcast. Easy on the eyes. No squinting or losing the ball in the sun.

I'm on the blue team, and I'm going against Bree Holland, possibly the premier defender in the country. And the striker on the red team is Kelsey Daniels; she made the national pool last year. I know they're looking to compare us.

The horn blares and we jog it in. Game time!

The red team prepares to kick off, and I dance in place.

This is the biggest. This is the best. This is what I live for. I'm pumped. I've got springs in my legs, the energy of a thousand Snickers bars.

Tweet! They play a quick touch forward and boot it long. It ricochets between several players before settling at a blue defender's feet. We're in possession.

We work the ball, work the ball, short passes, switching sides of the field, swinging it right, left, right, left, then back.

I try to do all the right things, all the little things. Run into space. Take my player away, then come back to show for the ball. Anticipate.

I make a diagonal run toward the flank as our wide midfielder receives the ball. Realizing she's one on one, I peel away to the far post to give her room. She beats her mark to the inside and shoots a shot that doesn't even penetrate their back line. Their sweeper tries to clear the ball, but miss-hits it. It's a line drive coming right at my face from about twenty feet away!

This could hurt, but I'm standing at the edge of the box. I jump and absorb the shot with my chest, dampening its power, caving in around it.

The ball settles at my feet. I get Matilda in my sights, plant, cock, and let it rip.

The way I connect, I can just tell. The ball rockets off my foot and knuckles towards the goal—an absolute laser. The goalie shifts left, then right, crouching low, hands out to either side.

It zings past her left shoulder and she's left standing flat-footed. Didn't even lunge for it.

I try not to smile too big as the team converges on me.

"Well done!

Good job!"

Seven minutes into the game and we're up one-nothing.

We give up our first goal. They score off a restart at the fif-teen-minute mark, and momentum tips their way. We can't seem to get the ball over midfield.

I'm getting impatient. I can feel it; I'm golden. Come on, defense. Give me that ball.

I gamble on intercepting a pass I have no business going for. I get a toe on it, just barely, but enough to deflect it. I'm way out of position, but we've gained possession.

No time to congratulate myself; Bree's on my back. She's riding my hip, tugging at my jersey. I shield the ball, jostle to keep position, and throw a few hip fakes. She doesn't fall for any of them.

Nutmeg her, I think, but I've got no time to turn and try. She's no dummy; she'll close up. So I heel it through her legs instead and curl off around her.

"Go with it!" someone shouts.

"Take it all the way to goal!"

But I don't. I pass off and bust to get back in position before everybody on the team hates me. I've gotten a goal, I've inter-cepted a pass, and I 'megged Bree. Now it's time to cool it, see if I can't set somebody else up.

But that doesn't last long. My teammates keep sending me balls. Our center midfielder chips me a beauty, lofting it over Bree's head, leading me so perfectly I don't even break stride. There's one red girl between the goalie and me. Like any good defender, she angles her stance, channeling me left. But she hasn't done her homework very well. She can't give me left; no one can. Because I'll take it.

I take the ball with my left for a few strides, touching it real unsure-like. Then I pause, straightening like I'm going to push it to my right.

The ball doesn't leave my left. It's a quick change of pace and a stutter step, no more. Nothing fancy. Just to relax her, then quick past her.

She's back on her heels trying to recover as I unload on the ball. At first it looks like my shot's high and wide. But there's so much English on that ball. It's curving . . . it's dropping . . .

It's bananas into the upper right!

I've been in the zone before, but never like this. I'm playing mindlessly. Can do no wrong. Everything's so easy.

I feel graceful. Almost lazy, as if to be getting these results I should be working harder, faster, more furiously. I know all these big-time coaches are watching, and that I'm on the same field with five or six girls who should leave my jaw hanging, but I feel like I'm all alone.

Ten minutes left in the half and the horn blows for a substitution. Blue team. A girl runs toward me. Me? Our bench coach nods and waves me in, pats me on the back. "Great job. Go get a drink."

I'm standing at the water cooler filling up a cup, privately reveling in the most awesome game of my life, when someone comes into my line of vision and gives me a thumbs-up.

Oh, my God! No way. Is that him? You bet your sweet bippy it is! It's Austin Gillingham, the North Carolina coach, and he's

113

smiling at me. Cold water splashes over my hand as my cup overflows.

I've run so fast I'm all out of breath. "Mom, hi, it's Leah. Let me talk to Dad!"

"Leah, Dad's in bad shape. He's taken a turn for the worse."

I swallow. "What happened?"

"We're not sure. He hasn't gotten out of bed all day. He's totally incoherent."

"You mean completely out of it?"

"Most of the time, yes. If he isn't sleeping, he's staring off into space or hallucinating. I caught him talking to the rocking chair today like it was Paul. I can't get him to eat or drink. I can't carry on a conversation with him."

"Does he ever snap out of it?"

"Sometimes he'll make sense for a minute or two, but then he loses it again mid-sentence."

"He's that different from the last time we talked?"

"Night and day. This morning he woke up scared and dis-oriented. He didn't know where he was. He couldn't see clear-ly, said his legs hurt. Heather came, and he was able to answer a few of her questions. Turns out he hasn't urinated in days. I feel so bad—I had no idea. He's been changing himself. I don't ask if he's gone or how many Depends he's wet. I checked the pack I bought him on Friday and he'd only used one of them. One, in four days!" Mom's voice cracks, "He never told me."

"Mom. It's not your fault."

It's quiet, then Mom sniffles herself together.

"Honey, we had to move him into the hospital bed. You should see how he thrashes about when he's hallucinating. And how he—oh Leah—I think you'd better come home."

CHAPTER 18

On the way home from the airport Paul tries to prepare me. "Don't be shocked if he doesn't recognize you. And don't be offended if he waves you away. Heather says it's withdrawal, part of the dying process."

"We don't know he's dying, Paul."

"Okay, Leah," Paul says condescendingly.

Then he changes the subject. "So how was it going in Colorado Springs?"

"Great. I was playing my best ever. I would have made that team, Paul."

"Maybe they saw all they needed to see."

I wish.

Mom leads us into the sunroom and I'm really scared I'm going to break down and be a mess in front of Dad. The room is crammed with stuff: a table on wheels, a TV and VCR, the walker and wheelchair, pillows, books, magazines, empty glasses. Gram, Mary, and Hugh are playing Scrabble at the foot of Dad's bed. It's like everyone is on sedatives—they're all whispery and sleepy-eyed.

Dad's eyes are half open and his lips are moving, but I think he's sleeping. He's very thin. Even with the sheets covering

116

him, I can see this. The dark, sunken hollows around his eyes. How small his neck is. The pronounced jaw and nose and cheekbones.

He startles and his eyes dart around. Without his glasses he looks so strange, nothing like my old Pops.

"You should put his glasses back on him, Mom."

"No," she says, "he falls asleep and rolls over on them."

His eyes. They're big, scared eyes, rolling around in their sockets. The skin has shrunken away from them, exposing so much more of the white than before.

I go over to the bed and hold Dad's hand. He smiles and says something in an airy voice I can barely hear, but then he says clearly, "How you doing, Weez?"

"Good, but I wish I'd gotten in on this game of Scrabble," I say clumsily.

"Don't worry, Weez, I'll deal you in on the next hand." Dad winks like he's up to something. It's good to see that familiar glint.

He names the people around the table in his mind, talking out the corner of his mouth as if they might hear him if he talks too loud. "See the guy with the brown curly hair? That's Dave Parker." Dad looks up at me. "Remember him?"

I have no idea who Dave Parker is.

Paul pulls me aside. "It's best not to play along with him. Heather says we should try to steer him back to reality. Say something like, 'We're not playing cards, Dad; we're playing Scrabble.' It humiliates him if he snaps out of it and realizes you've been talking to him like he's an idiot."

117

I look over at Dad, and he's still talking as if I were standing there. Even though he's so out of it, he looks peaceful. And he doesn't seem to be in any pain.

I'm standing over Dad during his first lucid moment since I've been home. He squeezes my hand and says, "Stand tall for your mother, okay, kiddo?" He winks at me.

Stand tall for Mom? I need somebody to stand tall for me.

I nod, my nose prickling. I'll try.

He gets upset and starts to cry, too. I put my head down next to his on the pillow so we can both hide our faces. "You're so brave," I whisper to him.

"Me? No, you're the brave one."

"No, I'm not," I squeak.

"Yes, you are. You're tough. And feisty. That's why they call you Weasel. . . . Weez? I want you to do me a favor . . ."

I nod. Anything.

"Promise me you—" He catches his breath and winces. "I could rest a whole lot easier if I knew you—" The pain grips him again.

I put my fingers to his lips—shhh, no more. For you, anything.

"I'm going to go take a look at Notre Dame, Dad."

"No, Weez, that isn't what I was going to say."

"Maybe not, but I'm going to make an official visit there. You never know."

"That would be great. But promise me one thing . . ." Dad pauses, his brow furrows. "Shoot, I forgot what I was going to say!"

I laugh—a belly laugh like I haven't laughed in ages—and Dad joins in. We laugh until we're crying again. Until we're weak. Until Dad falls asleep.

After a late dinner, Mom asks us to walk down to the beach with her—Mary, Paul, Gram, and me. Hugh stays with Dad.

We have a decision to make," she says. "And, Mom, like it or not, you're a part of this, too."

Gram nods.

"Dr. Ross called this morning. He thinks there's a blockage in the urinary tract. Left untreated, Dad will go into a coma and die within the week. All that backed up urea is poisoning him. Dr. Ross also said that there's a very fine line between what's done as a lifesaving measure and what's done in the name of providing comfort, and he feels we're on that fine line here."

"What does he mean by that?" I ask.

"Dad's signed a living will saying that no lifesaving measures are to be taken. But, technically, we would still be justified in doing something for Dad if it's being done, at least in part, to make him more comfortable. Dr. Ross said that's stretching it, though. He said Dad probably isn't even cognizant of pain anymore. It's been a couple days since he's complained of any."

"That's not true," I say. "I saw Dad wince tonight."

"You did?" cries Mom. "That's wonderful!"

We all laugh.

119

Mom blushes. "Anyway, Dr. Ross said it's a judgment call, and he'll leave it up to us."

"So what would they do to him?" asks Paul.

"Well, first they'd put a catheter in. If that doesn't help, there's another option, a relatively simple procedure. The doctors insert a scope that would make the entire urinary tract visible. If there's a blockage high up in the ureter, they'd insert a shunt at the point of blockage. The way Dr. Ross describes it, it's like a small section of drinking straw that would stand up to the pressure of the tumor and keep the ureter open. This can all be done without surgery, on an outpatient basis."

"Through the . . . ?" Paul cringes.

Mom nods. "Our third option is to do nothing, to let things progress naturally."

"Well? What do you think? We've got to make a decision by tomorrow morning, or it may be too late."

"He wants to see his grandchild," Mary says, looking at each of one of us for support.

Gram shakes her head and puts up her hands, pleading to be left out of it.

"Mary," Paul says, "he's signed papers saying no life-prolonging measures are to be taken. Legally, we have to honor that."

"But, Paul, is this a life-prolonging measure," says Mom, "or is it merely humane? You heard Leah; she saw him wince."

"Oh, come on, Mom, admit it; you want him to make it until Mary's baby is born. And who do you really want that for, him or Mary?"

"Paul, I admit I want him to see Mary's baby. Of course I do. I want that for all of us. Most of all for Dad. Maybe this will buy him a little time, give him a chance to meet his first grandchild. And to say a proper goodbye to his children."

Paul looks at me. "Leah. You have a say in this. What do you think?"

I think we should do anything we can to keep him alive, but then I remember that day when Dad told Heather he didn't want chemotherapy anymore, when he begged Mom to make him stick to his guns.

"I think you know him better than anybody, Mom," I say. "You know what he would want. I think you should decide."

I'm not sure if that makes it three against one with a no-vote from Gram, or if everyone just concedes their vote to Mom, but Mom says, "Let's try the catheter. If that doesn't work, we'll revisit our options. How does that sound?"

We all look at Paul.

"Everybody acts like I'm the fricking ice-man," he says. "Shit, I don't want Dad to die! But this isn't about me. This is about Dad and about what he wants. And he told us what he wants. He signed a living will!"

"He changed his mind once, Paul," says Mary, referring to Dad's decision to try the experimental chemotherapy. "Who's to say he won't change it again?"

When we go back in, we're all so exhausted that we get ready for bed right away. Mom asks me to sleep on the daybed with her, in the sunroom with Dad. We pull it out and make the pop-up bed I'm to sleep on. It's one, two, three across the sunroom—me, Mom, and Dad—three mattresses in a row.

CHAPTER 19

Friday, August 8

I squint at the curl of tubing in the weak gray light. It can't be six yet, but I've woken up one too many times to be able to put myself back to sleep. The urine's flowing in a slow but continuous stream, silently trickling down into the bag clipped to the side of the hospital bed. I watch it fill the bag, plumping it out and creeping up to the 800-ml line. Time to empty it. Again.

It's incredible. We must have emptied fifteen bags last night. When Heather put the catheter in yesterday the urine shot out like tap water under pressure. She had to drain the hose into a bucket instead of some little old bag. I bet Dad's lost thirty pounds, all water. All backed-up pee.

I'm glad the catheter's working and we won't have to weather another discussion with Paul about the outpatient procedure.

The tube moves, startling me out of my trance.

"Pops!"

"Weez?" he rasps. "Could you get me some water?"

"Sure." I've never been so happy to fetch anything in my whole life.

I thump Mom on the head. "Dad's awake."

She bolts up.

When I get back with the water, Mom's emptying the bag.

"Pete, this catheter saved your life. You have no idea. Do you remember any of it? Leah, his mind is clear! Can you believe it? We have him back!"

"You really scared us, Pops."

Mom pulls the sheet aside to check his legs. They're the scrawniest things I have ever seen. The knee is larger than the thigh and the skin hangs all wrinkly like an old man's. This is what's been underneath all that swelling? A leg can atrophy that quickly?

Mom quickly pulls the sheet over them.

"How do they look?" asks Dad.

"The swelling's down." Mom flashes him a smile, but her face has gone bone-white. "Leah, go get Paul and Mary and Grandma and tell them the good news."

Saturday, August 9

I go over and turn on the TV for Dad; Gram says there's a Packers game on he might enjoy.

"Turn that off," snaps Dad. "I'm so turned off by professional sports right now. Pro football!" he scoffs. "The way they pay those guys you'd think they were gods. Huh! You've got an ex-con out there, a wife beater, drug addicts. When I think of all that money, of all the good it could do . . ."

I wonder if he's turned off by soccer now, too.

Dad is so much better mentally, almost like his old self.

"Paul, get some paper," Dad orders. "I'm going to make a

list of everything I'd like you to do around here to get ready for winter."

I clear out of the sunroom to go fix myself a smoothie in the kitchen, where I can overhear their conversation without looking nosy.

"Dad, while you're making your list, there are some other things we need to talk about, too. Legal things, financial things."

Is that all that matters to Paul? Money?

"It's all taken care of," says Dad. "Everything's in the safety deposit box at the bank."

"Everything?"

"Yes. And I've thought about what to do with the restaurant. If you want it, it's yours."

Paul opens his mouth to talk, but Dad doesn't give him a chance. "Mary gets the jukebox; she's loved that thing since she was a kid. And you get the Minnesota Fats."

"No, Dad. It's worth way too much. Mom might want to sell it. Besides, where would I put it?" Paul's acting like he wouldn't think of taking that pool table. Give me a break. Everyone knows he's been lusting after that thing for ages.

"I'm sure you can figure something out. Buy yourself a bigger house. And Leah. I want Leah to have my Jeep. She's going to need a car when she goes away to college. Which brings up another point—her education. She'll probably get a scholarship, but just in case she doesn't, go ahead and sell the extra lot.

"The house is paid for. But it does need a new water heater. Both chimneys need to be cleaned. The gutter over the front door needs to be fixed. Get your mom set up with a plow service for the winter, if you would. Also, could you order a couple cords of wood and stack it where she can get to it easily? Oh, and I really want to put in an electric garage door opener for her."

Sunday, August 10

I stand on our beach watching the sunrise light up the opposite shore.

Let's see, what day is it? Saturday? No, Sunday. I heard a church service on Gram's TV this morning. Sunday, the last day of national camp. They'll all be flying out of Colorado today.

I start to run, just above the waterline where the sand is smooth and dark. I wish I could shake this feeling of being cheated.

Double-days start this week. Hard to believe it's the first time all summer I've even thought about it. When I was a freshman, it was all I thought of — getting to play high school soccer, trying out for varsity.

Hey, who's that? I'm coming up behind another runner. It looks like Kristin, the way the feet kick out to the side.

"Hey, Blaichek," I yell. "Wait up!"

She turns, jogging in place while I catch up to her.

"How's your dad?" she asks as we run in tandem.

"Pretty good. We had a real bad scare a few days ago, but he's okay now."

"That's good. Ready for double-days? They start Wednesday,

you know."

"I know." I don't dare tell her I haven't given it a thought until today. Still, I'm insulted that she'd think I'd forget. "I'm ready."

"Coach asked me to call and remind you, just in case, with all that you've been going through."

"What, are you kidding? Me forget double-days? Not on your life."

She laughs in a relieved kind of way and gets all gung-ho on me. "We've got to push hard, Weez; it's our last year. We're going all the way."

I wish I could believe that, but our high school team is a joke. Sure, we beat everybody around here, but we get creamed downstate. Not one of my teammates works on her game off-season.

Paul and Mary are preparing to leave when I get home.

"I hate to leave Daddy like this," Mary whispers, wrapping her arms around Mom's neck.

"Nonsense. You have a life of your own. You need to get back to it."

"But what if I never see him again!" Mary bursts into tears.

Poor Mary—all those hormones racing through her. "Don't worry," I say, hugging her. "He's doing so much better." She pats my head and gives me her crooked little dimpled-chin smile.

"Come on, Mary," says Hugh. "It's time for you to say good-bye to your dad."

She comes out twenty minutes later, all red and teary-eyed. She's out the front door and in the car so fast it's as if she's trying to outrun this goodbye.

Paul goes in as soon as Hugh and Mary are gone. He, too, comes out tear-streaked and mottled. He grabs a whole box of Kleenex on his way out the door. The Iceman has melted. It's twisted, the joy I feel seeing him this way, but it's nice to know he has a heart in there.

Mom and I collapse on the couch and cry until we are exhausted. Our eyes are scratchy and red and swollen. Her head must be pounding as hard as mine.

The phone rings as we're blowing our noses clear. Mom looks at me, begging.

I drag myself to the kitchen.

"Hello."

"Hi, this is Austin Gillingham from the University of North Carolina. Could I speak with Leah, please?"

Austin Gillingham! I want to pull back my listless hello.

"This is Leah,"

"Well, hello, Leah. How's your father?"

"He's okay. A little better."

"That's good to hear. I'm sorry for what your family's going through, though. And I don't mean to be a nuisance at a time like this, but I wanted to tell you how impressed I was with your play in Colorado. It was a shame you had to leave early. If I was picking that team, you'd be on it."

"Thanks." So that means I didn't make it.

"Leah, I'm very interested in you. Where you go to college is probably the last thing on your mind right now, but in case it helps to ease some of your uncertainty about the future, know that an education at the University of North Carolina is here waiting for you if you want it."

I hang up and stand with the phone in my hand, dazed. Was that a scholarship offer to North Carolina? I think it was.

"Who was it?" asks Mom.

"Oh, just some coach."

I'm so excited I could scream, but somehow excitement doesn't seem like an appropriate emotion to show right now.

CHAPTER 20

Wednesday, August 13

First day of double-days. Girls are on the lower field, boys on the upper. Same as always, the boys kicking their balls over the fence so they can come onto our field to get a closer look. Clay's never done it before, but he might be desperate at this point. It's been a couple weeks since he's seen me.

Sometimes I catch him looking at me. Or I feel it. Just like he looked at me that day in the boat. I keep my face steely and try to look impressive so he'll see I'm doing just fine without his help. My personal trainer. Right.

I sneak a look up there myself during water break. The boys are scrimmaging. Clay's doing pretty well. He needs to get rid of the ball quicker, though. I wish I could tell him that.

"My favorite part is when they do a wall and stand with their hands crossed over their crotch."

I cough up my water and spin around. It's Rebe Holleran, roving midfielder and team snoop. "What's the matter—you two have a spat?"

I look at her sideways like I don't know what she's talking about.

"You and Clay," she says. "I heard you two don't do anything together anymore. You used to be tight, didn't you?"

"Until he got weird on me. Why? Who'd you hear that from?"

"One of the guys. I hear Clay's really bummed out about it."

I wipe my mouth on my sleeve and dribble back out onto the field.

Yeah, me too.

When I get home after the second session, Gram's ducking out of the kitchen with something in her hand.

"You're not going to join us for dinner tonight?" Mom asks her.

"I don't have much of an appetite no more." She turns to Mom, but her eyes look at the floor. "I can't eat the way youse two do, sitting at the foot of that hospital bed with all them medical supplies everywhere. I'd rather take a sandwich into my bedroom."

"Looks like it's you and me tonight, Leah," says Mom.

Even though Dad's much better, he still doesn't want to eat. He forces down a couple teaspoons of Jell-O or yogurt because his pills are crushed in it and he can't get them down any other way, but that's it, every day. He tries to sit up in bed at mealtimes and at least watch us eat, though.

Mom sits down, Dad says the prayer with us, and we're off.

Someone brought over whitefish filets today. I love whitefish. I eat mine, Gram's, and part of Mom's.

"Have another piece of fish," says Dad.

I blush, but I tease him right back. "Stop it. You're just jealous."

It must be hard for Dad to watch someone eat like this. You'd think he'd be starving; he's eaten practically nothing this past week. Whenever we ask him if he wants something, he gets irritated. "Why do you keep asking me," he says, flashing those eyes, "when you know I don't feel like eating?"

Heather says we shouldn't pressure him. But I keep cooking things like cookies and pizza in hopes that he'll be unable to resist. I bring home rocky road ice cream, his favorite. Not even a spark of interest.

I can't believe a body can go on with so little fuel, but Heather says people can survive on just water for forty to sixty days.

I wonder how much time that leaves Dad.

Thursday, August 14

I was so tired this morning. Bleary-eyed, feet-dragging tired. I don't know why. Mr. Pfieffer's practices are so easy compared to ODP or club practices. But I slogged through the whole two hours. And I'm still tired.

I lie on the daybed and close my eyes. It feels so good.

"Weez," says Dad. "Do you feel like playing some cribbage?"

Not really. I stifle a sigh and hoist myself up. "Sure, Pops. Do you need your glasses?"

"Yeah. Yeah!" He says it like he's forgotten all about them and it just dawned on him.

"That's better," says Dad. "Now I can see. I think that was half my problem!"

He's gaunt and gray, but he looks so much better. He's my old Pops again, wearing his photo grays.

The play is pretty brisk—as brisk as cribbage gets—but I keep yawning.

"Don't do that," says Dad. "It's contagious. I'm tired enough."

I break out into another huge one, my jaws opening wider and wider.

"What, am I that boring?" snaps Dad.

It's ridiculous. I finish one yawn and another one's right behind it. My eyes are so watery I can hardly see.

"What's the matter? Pfieffer working you too hard?" There's no pity in Dad's voice. "Shit, what I wouldn't give just to walk again."

"You will, Pops. You'll see. You're so much better already."

It's true. Everyday since Paul and Mary left, he's gotten a little better. He won't eat, but he stays awake most of the day. And he's sharp. I don't know what's worse: when he's totally out of it, or when he's aware of everything and frustrated.

After our second session, I drag myself into the house. Mom must have heard the screen door slam; she comes into the kitchen and gives me an accusing look, one eyebrow down. I raise my hand, pleading guilty.

"Tough day, huh?" She pours me a glass of lemonade, and before I can even get my lips on it, she shoves a catalogue in my face. "Do you like this outfit?"

"I'd never wear it, but it would look good on you."

"Look through here and see if there's anything you like."

"Mom, right now I could care less about clothes."

"But what about new school clothes?"

"Mom, I'm too tired."

We hear a clank and run into the sunroom. Dad is sitting up in bed, wrestling with the side rail.

Sitting up?

Next thing you know he's put the rail down.

"What are you doing?" asks Mom.

"Got to get my stamina back." Dad pulls the sheets aside, freeing his legs. His knobby legs. His feet and knees are huge; the rest has withered away.

He swings his legs over the edge of the bed. Well, swings is hardly the word for it; his legs are so stiff he has to move them with his hands.

Dad sits there a minute, catching his breath, blinking, rubbing his eyes. I don't know what he's up to, but I sure wish he'd lie down.

Mom puts a guiding hand on his elbow, "Here, let me help you, Pete."

"I don't want any help," he snaps. "Go do something. I'm fine. I'm just going to take my time. Don't worry about me."

"What is it you're trying to do?" says Mom.

Dad ignores her. Holding onto the bed, he slides his bottom off the bed until his toes touch the floor. The way he's shaking, something's bound to give out. But then he's up. He's trembling and holding onto the steel bedrail, but he's standing.

"Get the wheelchair," he says to me.

This is the first time in a week he's been able to sit up, and now he's trying to get out of bed?

"Leah, get me the wheelchair."

I don't think this is such a good idea. But it's also not a good idea to argue with him right now, so I go and get it.

It's like slow motion, watching Dad lower himself into the wheelchair. Shaking and sweating, he lets go and falls the remaining six inches into the seat.

He did it. His back is bent, his chest is heaving, and his face is colorless mask, but he did it.

Who am I to be tired today?

CHAPTER 21

Monday, August 18

It's too early to get up, but there's no way I can sleep with all that clanging. Dad is fumbling around in his bed, rattling the side rails.

Mom's awake now, too, and she asks him what he's doing.

"I'm just going to get cleaned up," he whispers and winks at us like he's the boss again—we should go back to sleep and pay him no mind—he's got everything under control.

It's no big deal for him anymore. All it took was that first time to boost his confidence. He's still not eating, but he's stronger. I don't know how he can be, but he is.

This makes five days in a row he's gotten into his wheelchair by himself. Yesterday he did it three times. Each time he travels a little farther. He sits with Mom and me during dinner. Now that he can get around, he's tending to himself again. Mom set him up in the back hall where there's a laundry sink, a toilet, and room on the dryer for toiletries and a vanity mirror.

Dad comes wheeling back into the sunroom, clean-shaven except for the bloody dot of Kleenex on his chin. His bag is empty and his hair is combed. He gives me a big smile. I wish

Mom were here to see him—he's like a proud kindergartner ready for school pictures—but she's in the bathroom.

He looks so good maybe he'll feel like eating something today.

"Pops, do you want something to eat?" I ask.

He shakes his head and wrinkles up his nose. "No, thanks."

He's in a good mood, so I push it. "Nothing? Come on, there's got to be something. What do you say—what are you dying to sink your teeth into?"

"You know, I could go for some watermelon, maybe."

I can't believe it. I jump at it. "I'll go get you some before practice. Right now. Can I use the car?

"No. I don't want your mother to hear you going. This is our little secret. I don't want her to think I'll eat for you, but not for her."

"I'll ride my bike up to Michigan Traders."

Michigan Traders is a small twenty-four-hour mini mart. They don't carry much produce, so I've got my fingers crossed the whole way.

I hop off my bike and bulldoze through the door. There it is! In the ice chips against the far wall, a quarter of a seedless watermelon. The only one.

I'm making a b-line for it when who comes into the store but Clay. My heart jumps at the sight of him. A sickening hot flush surges through me.

I duck into an aisle, grab the first package I touch (hoping it's not a box of condoms) and pretend to read the side panel. My cheeks are flaming and my heart's a car idling out of control.

"Leah?"

No.

"Long time no see."

"I know."

"How are your double-days going?"

"Good. Yours?"

"Great. How's your dad?"

"Okay."

"I've been thinking about him a lot."

"Thanks. I'll tell him." I wave and put my head down, like I'm ready to go, but I don't. All I can do is stand there, stupidly frozen. Do I squeeze past him and get the watermelon, or do I just turn and leave?

"Did you get my letter?" he asks.

"What letter?"

"Oh, come on, you really didn't get it?"

"Nope."

"Unbelievable." He coughs. "The postal service can't even get a letter across town. I did write you a letter. And I did send it."

I raise my eyebrows.

"Nothing big. I just wanted to make sure that you were okay. You are, aren't you?"

"I'm fine."

"That's good. I'm glad. Hey, listen, call me sometime if you ever feel like talking."

He gives a stiff wave, looks down, and passes me wide in the narrow aisle, brushing against a pyramid of stacked Coke cans. It quivers and sways, on the verge of toppling. Clay steadies it, turns, and bolts out the door.

Coward. Clumsy coward.

Cute, sweet, clumsy coward. I want to run after him.

But I have to buy this watermelon.

As I'm lifting it out of the ice, I think, I could go right now and catch him pulling out.

Maybe not.

I could chase after him on my bike.

No, I'd look like a fool. And what would I say to him, anyway?

I stand in line at the register and watch Clay zoom down the road.

I could kick myself for letting him get away.

"Your mother's taking a shower," Dad says, and we smile at each other. We both know how long it takes her to do her hair.

I cut the melon into bite-sized pieces and watch him pop one piece after another into his mouth. I stare at him, overjoyed.

"Mmm, this hits the spot." He closes his eyes and shakes his head slowly back and forth. "That is the sweetest watermelon ever."

When he's done eating, a huge burp erupts from him, and we both laugh. Then he burps again, but it's not so funny this time because I can tell by his face that it hurts. He holds his stomach like he's going to throw up and burps and burps, each burp wracking his frail body. On top of this he's got the hiccups.

"Can you help me get back to bed?" Dad croaks.

Well, for five minutes he was happy. It was worth it, I rationalize. But I feel terrible for upsetting his stomach.

Dad lies back against the pillows, looking green. "Is there any of that watermelon left? If not, you go back and get me more tomorrow, okay, Weez?"

I smile and nod.

It was definitely worth it.

"Leah, come look at this," Mom whispers. Dad is sleeping.

"What?"

She points at Dad's bag.

"Ew." The urine is brownish red. "Why is it like that?"

Mom pulls me out into the kitchen. "It's blood in the urine. That's what Heather says."

"What does that mean?"

"Well, she's not sure. She said it could be an infection, bladder or kidney. She came and took cultures. We'll get the results back tomorrow."

"So what do we do now?"

"Watch. Wait. Hope it clears up. There was so much more than usual in his bag last time I emptied it, too. I don't know how that can be—he hasn't been drinking much."

CHAPTER 22

Tuesday, August 19

We're waiting for Heather to arrive with the results. The bag of urine is still filling up rosy, and Dad's not so good.

"I'm a little tired this morning," he says. "I think I'll just lie here and convalesce for a while."

Convalesce? No, Pops. I want to shake him and yell: Get up! You're getting stronger, remember? You can't break your string now. Today would make it six days in a row! But he's been real sleepy since yesterday, hasn't shown any interest in the wheelchair at all.

If Heather doesn't get here soon, I'll have to go to practice and miss hearing what she has to say. I always get the feeling that Mom softens the news when she relays it to me.

Heather sits us down before even checking on Dad. "We're stumped. The cultures don't show any infection. Dr. Ross suspects kidney failure, but with that, there's a usual progression, the first signs being heavy output and clear urine. The blood in the urine is a mystery. If it is kidney failure, you'll see a sudden decrease in output soon. Then it will taper off until there's none, and he wouldn't have much time left after that."

"It's not kidney failure," I blurt out.

Mom and Heather look at me.

"That's right. It's not kidney failure, and whatever's wrong is all my fault. I gave him some watermelon."

"Watermelon?" says Mom. "When? Where did you get watermelon?"

"At Michigan Traders, while you were in the shower yesterday."

"How much did he eat?"

"About half a quarter. An eighth."

"That's an awful lot of watermelon for a man who hasn't eaten in over a week!" She looks at me and then at Heather, aghast.

"Watermelon is a diuretic," says Heather. That would account for the increased output, but it doesn't explain the blood in the urine." She laughs her tinkly little laugh. "Don't worry, Leah, it's not your fault. It's definitely blood and not watermelon juice."

On my way home at noon, I stop to see if I got any more letters from colleges. I pull up to the mailbox, straddling my bike, and sift through the pile of envelopes and junk mail.

What? Another letter from Clay? I throw my bike down and rip it open.

> Dear Leah,
>   It was good to see you at the store yesterday. I wish we could talk. I didn't think our little argument on the phone a couple weeks ago was

anything to get so upset about.

We are too good of friends to let something like that get between us.

I'm here if you ever need me. I miss you.

Love, Clay

I miss you? I'm here if you ever need me? Oh, please, spare me.

I'm about to tear the letter to shreds, like I did his last one, when a car beeps. It's Enzo, turning into our drive. He rolls down his window and says, "I was just coming to visit your dad. Want a ride down?"

"No, I've got my bike." I point to the heap under the mailbox. "Thanks."

When I've got myself together about Clay's letter, I ride down and join Mom, Dad, and Enzo in the sunroom. Mom's got the sheet pulled down over the urine bag so no one can see it.

We have a good visit with Enzo. He's brought us sandwiches from the restaurant for lunch, and while Mom and I eat, he tells jokes and fills Dad in on everything at the restaurant.

Right after Enzo leaves Dad falls asleep. I go over and peek under his sheet. Same rust-colored urine as this morning. And lots of it.

CHAPTER 23

Wednesday, August 20

You'd think I had a dentist appointment this morning, the way I'm dreading this. Geez, I'm tired. Bone tired.

It's getting harder and harder to go to practice these days. It's not just that I'm tired. And it's not just that I have to face Clay. Worse than that is this gut feeling I have that I should be home right now.

Mom's all alone. Well, not really, but Gram's no help. And Dad's going downhill again. This blood in the urine is freaking us out.

But I go to practice anyway, and once I'm there and get into the flow of things, I almost enjoy it. I can tune Clay out, I can forget about Dad. I can lose myself in the drills and the scrimmages.

Saturday, August 23

We've got our first scrimmage this afternoon, against Ludington, so we've got the morning off. I sleep in late, and then I hang around the house eating, reading, and talking with Mom and Dad. I even challenge the hermit to a game of Scrabble. Poor Gram. Sometimes it's easy to forget she lives here.

I yawn and look at the clock. Time to get ready.

Uncurling from the wicker chair, I rise slowly, arching my back, stretching.

After sitting around all morning, I could use a good workout. And Ludington will give us one. They're a bunch of wealthy downstate transplants who've grown up playing on club teams that have the luxury of hiring the best coaches, playing on the best fields, and traveling to the best tournaments. So they're a little soft, but they're polished.

I can't remember the last time I went to a match alone, no one coming to watch me or pick me up. No Mom, no Dad, no Clay. It was like that in Colorado, but that was different. Everyone was alone there.

"Ready, Weez?" Kristin offers her hands up high. "Come on, let's go get these Ludington pansies."

Pansies? First play of the game I'm taken out by a vicious slide tackle. No whistle. That pretty much sets the tone for the game.

Two plays later, this girl practically rips my jersey off. These Ludington girls are not quite as soft as I remembered.

Funny how sometimes you can't adapt to the situation. You know the ref's letting a lot go. You know you should start dishing it out yourself. But you don't.

I don't feel like playing nasty. I want to play nice, clean soccer today, to knock the ball around and lose myself in the flow of the game.

Coach Pfieffer gives it to us during half time. "Where is your intensity?" he yells. "Ludington is out-hustling us. They've won every fifty-fifty ball. Every single one!" He's talking a million miles an hour. Spit's flying. "You've got to show me you want it! Show me you've got some heart! Show me some passion!"

Passion? Heart? Sounds like a religious experience.

"Dig deep, ladies. Show me you've got some guts." Coach Pfieffer's red in the face, pounding his fist into his hand with every syllable. He acts like this is a matter of life and death.

Well, let me tell you something, Mister—this is nothing. If you want to know about life and death, come on over to my house. Then we can talk about guts and intensity and digging deep.

"You've got to have desire! You've got to be willing to sacrifice your body!"

Sacrifice my body? Not on your life. We only get one body, Mister, and this is just a game.

"Play like this is the last game you'll ever play!"

It just might be. The last game I play, that is.

How did I ever listen to this stuff before? How could I have ever bought into it? I mean, if everyone would just shut up and play, I could handle it, but I can't take all the motivational speeches and rah-rah stuff anymore. This is not that important; it's just a game.

I wait in the locker room until everyone's gone, and then I

walk up to Coach Pffiefer as he's pulling up corner flags on the field.

"Coach? Can I talk to you?"

He turns, kind of startled. "Leah. Sure. What's up?"

"Well, you know about my dad, right?"

"Yes. How is he?"

"He's pretty bad."

"I'm sorry," he says, putting a hand on my shoulder.

"Yeah, we have to do everything for him and it's real hard on my mom. I feel like I should be at home now. I don't know, by the time I go to practice and come home each time, we're talking three hours. Three hours twice a day. That's six hours. I hate the thought of quitting but—"

"Whoa, whoa, quitting? Wait a minute. Let's talk about this, Leah. In less than two weeks we'll be down to one practice a day."

"But then I'll be in school all day."

"Oh. Right." Coach Pfieffer's brow furrows. "Hey, I understand. I do. I just think that your teammates' support is something you could really use right now. And you'd miss it. You'd miss soccer."

"I know. But right now it's just another source of stress for me. I'm so exhausted I hardly make it through practices. Whether I'm physically tired or emotionally tired, I don't know. But my heart isn't in it anymore."

"I understand, Leah. I just want you to be sure you've thought this through. We'll all hate to see you go. But don't worry; nobody's going to think you're a quitter. You stay home if that's where you need to be right now. Your spot will always be here waiting for you."

CHAPTER 24

Monday, August 25

It's a beautiful afternoon and Mom's cutting Dad's hair on the deck. His hair is thin from the chemo, but there's this fuzzy new growth pushing up from under the long, white hair. Mom waves me over to show me.

"Look, Leah. It's brown. Isn't that funny?"

The scissors flash in the sun as she clicks away at one side of his head. Curly wisps of Einstein frizz float to the redwood decking.

"You're going to feel so much better after this, Pete. How long has it been since your last haircut? You've even got mutton chops."

Dad's patient, but his jaw muscles are twitching, and I can tell he's had enough.

I hardly recognize him. I don't know if it's the haircut or if it's because he's lost so much weight in his face, but his ears look huge and they stick way out from his head. When Dad's not looking, I pull my ears out and make a face at Mom. We try not to laugh.

Mom and I are in such a giddy mood as we pick up the deck. Mom clowns around behind Dad, holding two fingers over his head as she vacuums his neck. I stifle a snicker, bend down, and busy myself sweeping up hair so Dad won't see my face. Out the corner of my eye I see Mom with her hand over her mouth, her face bright red, and my insides turn to Jell-O.

It's like getting the giggles in church. I bite the inside of my cheeks and look down. If I look up at either of them, I'll burst out laughing. I know I will. And we can't let Dad know how bad his haircut looks; he'd be so mad.

We help Dad back to the sunroom for a nap and scurry off to Mom's room, where we collapse on the bed and bust out, roaring and rolling around.

"Oh, ho, ho . . ." Mom's coming down from one of her shrill trills, holding her side with one hand and wiping her eyes with the other. "Did you see what I did to him?" She cracks up again.

"Mom, people are going to laugh at him!"

"I hope not! Oh, Leah, we can't let him get anywhere near a mirror."

I explode, snorting out of my nose at the thought of Dad's fury if he were to see what Mom did to him.

"What?" says Mom. "What's so funny now?"

"We're afraid of a ninety pound weakling!" I can barely get the words out, I'm laughing so hard.

Mom is purple, jiggling and pounding the bed with her fist. "Oh, this feels so good! Let's not stop! Tell me something else!"

"Did I tell you what happened yesterday while you were out walking?"

"No, what?"

"Get this. Dad calls me to his side like he's got something

150

really important to say, so I hustle over. He asks me to get him a board, three feet long. So I hurry out to the garage and find a piece of wood. I measure it, cut it, and bring it back to him, dying to know what he could possibly want it for. He looks at me like I'm crazy and says, 'What the hell is this for?'"

Mom throws her head back and laughs—a big, free, ha-ha of a laugh.

"It's strange, isn't it, how his mind's been affected?" She dabs at her eyes. "Yesterday I brought him a glass of water with a straw in it and he looked at it and said, 'Do I blow or suck?'"

"Wow. That's like when he was trying to open that little jar of lip balm. He sat there staring at the lid for the longest time and finally he asked, 'How do I get this off?'"

Mom starts to laugh, then puts a hand to her lips. "Sometimes I don't know whether to laugh or cry. Maybe I'm warped, but there is something really comical about all this, isn't there?"

"There is. You have to laugh about it. Did you hear what he said to Mary? She was feeding him chicken noodle soup and the noodles kept slipping out of his mouth. So she's picking all these noodles off his chest and dabbing at him with a napkin, and he looks up at her and says, 'Mary. Please. Just let the noodles fall where they will.' In this real serious, professor-like tone."

Mom shakes her head and smiles. "How about the day he used the word convalesce? He's never used words like that!"

"Yeah, it's weird. His vocabulary seems to be growing. Did you hear him the other day when Enzo was over?"

"No, what?"

"Well, we must have been talking too loud, because Dad said, 'Would you all please disperse for a while?'"

"Oh, yes, disperse! How could I forget?" Mom slaps her knee. "Did you notice how he calls me Rita now, too, instead of Mumma? In the twenty-eight years we've been married he's never called me by my name, and all of a sudden I'm Rita. It sounds so formal coming from him."

"That's the thing; it's not so much what he says as how he says it. Like he's trying to impress us, to be so civilized despite everything's that's happening to him."

"I know. He tries so hard." Mom smiles a crooked smile and her chin trembles. "These things, they're really not as funny as they are pathetic. We must be pretty desperate if this is all we have to laugh about."

In less than thirty seconds, Mom's gone from laughing to crying. The tears never stop flowing for long. It's exhausting. As fast as everything has happened this summer, living it is some kind of slow torture.

Friday, August 29

Jack Murphy, Dad's golfing buddy, is sitting on the daybed drinking a beer and talking about the time he took Dad hunting in the Upper Peninsula.

"So we're behind a tree and this deer comes into the clearing and just stands there. It's a beautiful buck, an eight-pointer. 'It's yours, Petey,' I whisper to him."

It's a story we've heard Mr. Murphy tell a hundred times,

but we always enjoy it. Mr. Murphy is loud and funny, very theatrical. His deep bass voice even draws Gram out of her bedroom.

"Mrs. Weiczynkowski!" He takes both of her hands in his. "You look wonderful."

Gram waves him away and blushes. She loves Mr. Murphy's flattery. It even earns him the can of cashews she's been stashing somewhere in the kitchen.

"Why, thank you, Mrs. W." He pats the daybed for Gram to sit down. "Anyway, the buck's in the clearing, frozen, staring straight at us. Pete lifts his gun and gets the deer in his sights." Mr. Murphy is up now, acting it out. "But he doesn't shoot. He puts the gun down and says, 'I can't. He's looking me right in the eye.' So we let that sucker go!" He laughs like thunder rolling. "Do you remember that, Petey?"

Dad smiles and nods.

"Your dad's no hunter, Leah, that's for sure. I never invited him again."

Mr. Murphy talks about golf games, outrageous bets, foolish arguments, trips he and Dad made downstate for Lions games, all that nostalgic stuff Dad loves.

He certainly has a way of lifting Dad's spirits.

Mr. Murphy's not the only one. More and more people come everyday. I can't believe how many people care. They bring cookies, cakes, baskets of fruit, warm casseroles. Betty Schmidt from church brings him Communion when Father Pat can't. Enzo comes almost every day to play cards with him.

Dad rallies for their visits and holds up amazingly well, but as soon as they leave, he crashes. Sometimes all the company gets to be too much for Dad, and we have to ask people to come back another time.

But it's not just the visitors. The phone rings non-stop, everyone wanting to know how Dad is. People from far away who just found out, Dad's brothers, Mary and Paul.

Speaking of Paul, he should be here any time now. He left work right after lunch and is going to stay through Labor Day to work on that list of things Dad gave him to get the house ready for winter.

Saturday, August 30

All afternoon Paul hustles around, dirty and sweaty and dressed in clothes the likes of which I've never seen him in — a ratty old T-shirt and a pair of Dad's paint-splattered khakis.

Dad barks an endless stream of orders from his bed. I'm holding a ladder for Paul, and we can't help but hear him through the screen door. "Use the square brush in the chimney, not the round one. And when you're done with that, stack the wood on the deck."

"Okay, Dad," we say, and Paul winks at me as he lowers the round brush down the chimney.

Little does Dad know the wood has already been stacked — on the front porch, where it won't get wet. For the first time we can do things our own way and Dad can't come check.

Tuesday, September 2

Tick, tick, tick goes the rain against the window. It's so quiet in this house. Paul went home, and the lake is quiet again. It's September. The summer people have gone home to the city. Everybody's back to work, back to school.

Except me. It's the first day of school, and Mom hasn't even asked me why I didn't go. Neither has Dad; he doesn't even know what day of the week it is anymore. Nobody from school calls asking where I am. It's been weeks since the last college coach called. I guess it's an unspoken thing.

As nice as it is that no one's expecting anything of me right now, it's also kind of weird. It's like I don't exist to anyone outside this house. We don't go to church anymore. My soccer team plays on without me. I've cut myself off from Clay. And most of the time I like it that way.

I want to be here just for Dad. And Mom. They're all I have energy for. Mom and I are up and down all night, caring for Dad. Even when I do sleep, it's real light. I keep one ear cocked, listening to Dad's breathing. Sometimes it falters; I won't hear anything for a long time and then he puffs out with this huge breath he's been holding. He's always had sleep apnea, but not like this. Each breath seems like it could be his last.

I stand up and look out the rain streaked windows. You can't even see the lake today. Everything's fuzzy, foggy, steamy gray.

Labor Day. What a depressing holiday. Summer's over. Fall's begun.

I used to love fall—the beginning of soccer season, the

crunch of leaves, the smell of wood burning, Halloween, Thanksgiving, the first snow.

Now I hate it. Everything's coming to an end. Leaves will be falling, leaving bare stick branches. The landscape will go from green to red, yellow, and orange, and then to brown and gray, everything brown and gray. There'll be rain and mud, freezing winds, snow. And everything will die or go to sleep for the winter.

I grab yesterday's unread *Record Eagle* for something to do and flip through to the sports section. The headline reads TROJAN GIRLS CONTINUE TO DOMINATE WITHOUT THEIR WORKHORSE.

The article and two pictures—one of Coach Pfieffer and another of Kristin punching a ball away—fill the bottom half of the front page.

> The Traverse City Trojan girls' soccer team may have lost their star, All-American striker Leah Weiczynkowski, but they seem to be doing just fine without her.

It sure feels good to see my name in ink, even if they are doing fine without me.

> In the title match of the Northern Michigan Kick-Off Classic Friday, the senior high girls beat Alpena 5-0, clinching the tournament title for the fourth consecutive year. On Wednesday,

they similarly defeated a highly-touted Harbor Springs squad, 6-1, to advance to the finals.

Asked if he's surprised with the early victories and the ease with which they came, Trojan coach Ron Pfeiffer said, "Yes, I'm amazed. I really am. We're playing without our leading scorer (Weiczynkowski). Leah's accounted for ninety percent of our goals over the past three years. I never expected we could make up for her loss."

Weiczynkowski, who left the team shortly after preseason practices began to be at her father's side during his battle with cancer, is out indefinitely. "Her family needs her more than we do right now," said Pfeiffer. "For the time being, we're doing fine, far better than I could have hoped."

So, to what does this group of over-achievers attribute its success?

"We're a highly motivated team. We're on a mission this year," said senior co-captain and starting goalie Kristin Blaichek. "We're playing for Mr. Weiczynkowski."

It's true, said Pfeiffer. "They've really pulled together as a team. The younger girls are filling in the gaps nicely, and our veteran players have stepped up their level of play."

Even so, Pfeiffer misses Weiczynkowski's

leadership. "We haven't found a go-to player to take Leah's place," he said. "You know, that person you look to come up with the big goal in a pressure situation. So it'll be a little scary in the tight games. Leah's left some awful big shoes to fill."

I turn the page and there's a big picture of Dad and me standing in the parking lot of Pete's Place. I'm in uniform holding up a trophy, and Dad's arm is slung over my shoulder. It's from when we won the Kick-Off Classic my freshman year. We look so young! And so happy. I wonder who gave it to them.

I read the last bit of the article under the picture:

> Pfeiffer praised Weiczynkowski for her decision to forego playing to stay at her father's side, however. " It just goes to show what kind of a kid Leah is, that she would give up something she loves so much to be with her family. I hope she reads this and sees we're all behind her. We're dedicating this season to her dad, to Pete Weiczynkowski. All our efforts go in hopes that he'll beat this thing. Pete's one of our most loyal fans and supporters. We'd love nothing better than to see him feeling better, to get him back on his feet and out here to one of our games."

It makes me feel good to know they're thinking of Dad and me. But some of their comments irritate me, too. Like the part about Dad getting back on his feet again. As if there's any chance of that.

I guess they can't help it. Everybody's just trying to be nice. It's my fault I don't talk to any of them, or they'd know how Dad's really doing.

CHAPTER 25

Thursday, September 4

Jennifer's coming to spell us for a couple hours so Mom and I can take Gram to get her hair done this morning. While she's in the beauty parlor, as she calls it, Mom and I are going to take a long walk on the beach, and then we'll pick her up and go to the grocery store. Jennifer comes on Tuesday and Thursday mornings from ten until noon. It's the only chance we have to get away from the house.

As we're getting ready to leave, Jennifer undresses Dad for a sponge bath. She does it very slowly because it's painful for Dad to raise his hands high enough to pull the nightshirt off over his head. He hasn't been out of bed in a week now, not since the haircut, and his big shoulders have atrophied away to nothing more than ball and socket joints covered by skin. I can't believe the amount of muscle his frame was carrying. His barrel chest is gone now, too. He's all ribs and a sunken-in stomach with hipbones sticking out.

When Jennifer touches the warm washcloth to his chest, he recoils in pain.

"Sorry," she says, "I'll try to be gentle." He grimaces the whole while, tight-lipped, eyes closed.

Mom and I leave without interrupting to say goodbye. We

drop Gram off at Ruth's Beauty Salon and head for the beach.

We move out, matching each other step for step, left, right, left, right. I'm dying to break into a run, but I get the sense this is supposed to be a mother-daughter thing, so I decide to chill out and enjoy it.

A deserted beach lies in front of us. No people, no boats. No footprints, no trash, all the sand washed smooth by the rains. The sun is high and warm, and it feels like August. The only sound is a seagull squawking high overhead. Our own private, pristine beach.

"Mom, promise me we won't move."

She looks at me like I'm crazy. "Of course not. This is our home."

"I don't have to go to college right away. I can stay home and work at the restaurant for a while. I can help out."

"Don't be ridiculous. You're going to college." Mom marches straight ahead. "Leah, let's not plan too far ahead, okay? Everything will work out."

Mom doesn't like talking about the future.

We stride along the water's edge. Mom's pumping her elbows at her side, really putting her elbows into it, like she means business. I amble along leisurely next to my spazzy mother, my arms long and swinging.

It's so refreshing to be outside instead of cooped up in that house.

"Mom, you should ask Jennifer to come more often."

"No. If you were dying, you wouldn't like being taken care

of by a stranger. I feel bad enough leaving him for just these couple hours. But if you're needing to get out more, I can find people to take you places. Mandy's mom would be more than happy to help. She's offered to come get you so you can—"

"No way, Mom." Mandy's this girl who goes to our church. We carpooled to catechism, made our First Communion together, got confirmed together. So Mom thinks we're old buds, and whenever we see them at church, she and her mom are always trying to set something up between us. "Want to go to a movie Friday? Want to go bowling?"

"Well, what about Clay, then?" asks Mom. "He'd come get you and take you out. You haven't seen him at all lately, have you?"

"No, I told you, Mom, he's really just a training partner. If I'm not working out, I don't have a reason to see him."

"But you like him, right? Maybe you should give it a chance to be more."

"Listen, Mom. I wasn't asking you to figure out my social life for me. I just meant that I was enjoying this—this walk with you. Getting out of the house with you."

Mom tucks her chin and smiles. She blinks and wipes a tiny tear from her cheek—the woman is an absolute sieve. "Thank you, Leah. I'm enjoying it, too."

My arms are full of groceries and the screen door slams before I can catch it.

"What the hell!" Dad's glaring at me from the hospital bed.

"I was fast asleep. How many times have I told you not to slam that door?"

"Sorry, Pops," I say. "It was an accident."

Loud noises really bother him. So do strong smells and tastes. Some are not so loud or so strong, and still they bother him. He complains about the way I walk. "When you walk, the whole house shakes. I don't know why they call you Weasel; you walk like a herd of elephants." He doesn't like the sound of the mixer, either, or the smell of perfume. He says our water tastes funny.

"We got you some raspberry ginger ale, Pop," I say, trying to redeem myself. "Want some?"

"Yeah, get me a glass, would you, Weez?"

Dad may not eat, but he certainly drinks. A lot. Water, juice, ginger ale, Coke.

I bring him a glass of ginger ale with a couple ice cubes and a straw.

"Thanks." He props himself up on one elbow and takes the glass from me.

I keep my hand under it for a second because he's shaky and it looks like the glass might slip out of his hand, but he manages to keep hold and get the straw to his lips. His lips are tacky, though, and the tip of the straw sticks on his lip instead of going in far enough to drink. He reaches up to redirect it with his finger. I want to help, but he likes to do things for himself. When he finally gets the straw in right, he sucks long and hard, the fibers of his neck straining.

Heather takes the stethoscope out of her ears and stands up. She sighs and motions for us to follow her out in the kitchen.

I feel so morbid when Heather pulls us aside. It's like goody, goody, goody, what kind of gore have you got for us today? I can't get enough of these graphic updates and almost feel let down when she has nothing dramatic to tell us. It's so boring. Don't tell me he's the same; tell me awful things are oozing from his pump stoma and that he has a fever of a hundred and six and practically zero blood pressure. Now that's something to tell people when they call.

Don't get me wrong—I don't want Dad to suffer. I want him to get better, to feel good again, to be my old Pops. But that's not going to happen, and when day after day he lies in the same stale, unchanging state, it gets old. We're hanging in limbo, doing the slow torture. If something bad is going to happen, maybe we should get it over with.

"I'm pretty sure it's kidney failure now," Heather says. "It's not a classic case, but the lingering disorientation seems to indicate that the kidneys aren't filtering the wastes out of his blood like they should be."

"What about the ureter?" Mom says. "At one time you thought there might be a blockage there."

"No, the urine is getting out, so we're not worried about a blockage anymore. It's a filtering problem, which means it's the kidneys. But we still can't account for the blood in the urine. It could be that the tumor is ulcerating."

Ulcerating. The word paints an ugly picture.

"Do you think I should I call the kids home?" Mom asks. She bites her lip. "I guess Mary couldn't really come right now, but Paul could."

"I would. I don't imagine Pete has many lucid days left. They won't be able to carry on much of a conversation if you wait."

"I think Paul's said his goodbye, don't you, Leah?"

I nod, but I roll my eyes. Why is Mom being so cold? I can't believe she wouldn't call Paul and give him one last chance to talk face-to-face with Dad.

She must realize how she sounds because then she adds, "Last time they said goodbye it was so draining for him and Pete. I'd hate to see them go through that all over again."

"If you feel they've already said goodbye," says Heather, "and they just want to be here to support you and the family at the very end, then you can probably wait. You'll know when it's time. He'll put out amazing amounts of urine, and then it will decrease drastically, less and less until he slips into a coma. Then it's just a matter of days."

We watch the urine bag like a barometer. It's the first thing I look at when I walk into the sunroom. Is there more than usual? Less? Is it getting redder? Thicker?

Mom whispers to me when we're in the bathroom getting ready for bed. "Heather's notes in the hospice folder describe it as looking like tea. It's definitely deeper red than that now, opaque and thicker, too, don't you think?"

I gag as I spit out my fluoride rinse. "Yeah."

In her nightgown, Mom drains Dad's bag a final time for the night and dumps it in the back hall toilet. When she gets back, she jots down the time and amount in her notebook: 9:30 pm, 700-ml.

She sits at the glass table and figures the totals for the day, her pencil working carefully. I watch over her shoulder, anxious to see the results. Digit by digit, they appear as she adds the columns. No drastic increase, no drastic decrease; input matches output.

I approach the hospital bed, hesitant, wondering if this is my last goodnight, and what I should do if it is, what I should say to him that I haven't already said. Should I resist being maudlin, think positive, and plan on a hundred more goodnights? This is my nightly decision.

Dad's eyes are closed, but that's never a guarantee he's sleeping. I can't just skip saying goodnight. He'd notice. And though it seems callous to give him a quick kiss, like, So the urine still looks like tomato juice—I'm not going to get worked up about it, he knows what I'm doing if I linger or say anything beyond "I love you." He hangs onto my hand, squeezing it, and turns his face away so I won't see him cry.

Poor Dad. There's no place for him to hide anymore.

I hurry over, bend down, and give him a quick peck on the cheek. "See you tomorrow morning, Pops."

His eyes stay closed, but he smiles. "Night, Weez. Love you."

"Me, too," I say. And I'm real proud of how well this goodnight went.

CHAPTER 26

Saturday, September 6

Mom and I are sitting at Dad's side, reading to him. He says he can't focus his eyes anymore; they skip all over the page. We hear footsteps outside and through the wall of windows we see Mrs. Kreegan coming up the back porch steps. Dad is lying here with just his nightshirt on, knees drawn up so that all of him is exposed from the waist down. Mom takes the sheet from where it lies crumpled at his feet and pulls it over him.

Dad kicks the sheet aside. "I know my body disgusts you," he says, grabbing at the emaciated ruins of his thighs, his big-boned mitts encircling them almost completely, "but I'm hot."

Doesn't Dad see Mrs. Kreegan coming up the walk? He's looking that way. But who knows what he can see anymore.

"Oh, Pete, your body doesn't disgust me," says Mom, gently rubbing his thighs.

His legs are very thin, but not at all disgusting. There's still a lot of muscle hanging on them, lean and sinewy now, rather than thick and rounded. And the way it hangs in tight, shrunken bundles on those long thin bones, there's a certain grace about them, like a track star's legs.

"Mrs. Kreegan is here," says Mom, covering him again. "I

don't know how comfortable she'd be with seeing so much of you."

During the visit, Dad is restless. Whether he means to or not, he squirms until he's kicked the sheet down, until he's lying there with everything hanging out again. But he's more comfortable. And it's okay how it happens; it's such a slow, painstaking effort, him reaching down and fumbling to move the sheet lower, kicking at it with his stiff legs, that I think Mrs. Kreegan has time to get comfortable with it—with his nakedness, with the pump stoma, the catheter, and the trickle of red urine dripping into the bag.

Somehow it's not gross. It just seems natural. This is the way Dad is. There should be no secrets anymore.

Sunday, September 7

We hear Dad whimpering and run over to his bed. He's holding his lower back and writhing.

"What is it, Pete?" asks Mom. "What's wrong?"

"My back." Dad grits his teeth and squeezes his eyes shut. "The pain . . ."

Dad rolls in bed, moaning. "I don't know what to do! Help me." He tosses and turns, face scrunched, head back, grunting and holding his breath like a woman in labor. It's terrible to watch, like something is eating him from the inside, taking big, cruel bites.

"Leah, get the Roxanol." Mom points me to the kitchen.

"But he just had some."

"I don't care!" Mom's face is screaming even if her voice isn't.

"No." Dad shakes his head. "No drugs. Just get me a cigarette."

"A cigarette? You haven't smoked since Leah was born."

"Go get me a cigarette! In the hutch. Top drawer on the right."

Mom raises her eyebrows at me, and I run to get the cigarette and some matches.

His body's frozen, but he's rolling his head from side to side, squeezing his eyes shut against the pain. I light the cigarette and put it between his trembling fingers. He takes a hard, desperate drag on it. But his nostrils curl and he hands it right back to me. "Take this away. Pray with me. See if that helps."

Mom and I hold his hands. "Our Father, who art in heaven, hallowed be Thy name . . ."

When we're finished with that, Mom opens the Bible and leads me with her finger through Dad's favorite passages, which we read fast and furiously.

We read and read.

The prayers seem to help. Dad calms down and his face relaxes.

"That was the worst pain I've ever felt. Burning, stabbing." His voice is a whisper. He doesn't even open his eyes. "It lasted so long."

"You must be exhausted," says Mom. "That was at least ten minutes. Leah, go get him a glass of water."

I do. He drinks the whole thing at once and opens his eyes

to look up at us for the first time.

"Isn't there anything we can do to speed up this process?" he asks, eyes pleading.

Mom sighs. "Well, you know about Kevorkian," she says matter-of-factly. "And you know that it's a common but illegal practice that some doctors advise family members on how to turn up the morphine drip if their loved one wants to go. They do it quietly when no one is in the room. The person just drifts off, and no one is the wiser."

I'm afraid Mom is going to ask Dad how he feels about that, but she doesn't. She tells him how she feels instead.

"I think that, hard as it is, suffering has a purpose and ought to be endured to the natural end. What purpose, I'm not sure. Maybe it's for you, the person suffering, to come to terms with the pecking order of the universe, to reach a certain level of spirituality that you never would otherwise. And for us, the ones watching you suffer; we've learned so much from how you've handled this, Pete. You've been so brave, so uncomplaining and selfless, worrying about what's going to happen to all of us instead of dwelling on your own pain and fears. I've grown spiritually just watching you."

I grab Dad's hand and nod. I've grown, too.

When Dad falls asleep, Mom and I look at each other like the parents of a colicky baby who has finally dozed off.

"Go running," Mom whispers. "Get out while you can. It's so beautiful out. I'll stay with Dad."

"What about you? Why don't you get a walk in?"

"I'll go when you get back. Go. Don't waste this chance."

I steal away and go for a run on the peninsula.

It's a shimmering afternoon — the sun, the water, the breeze in the leaves — and I head for the hills. The peninsula has these great rolling hills covered with orchards, open meadows, patches of woods. I like to follow the farmer's tire ruts in the meadows between the orchards. This is what Laura Ingalls Wilder's prairie must have looked like. A rippling, undulating sea of grass, bleached golden from the summer sun, all heathered and feathery like it's been painted with an airbrush.

It's more than just grass, though. As I leave the tire ruts to head straight for the peak of the hill, I see that it's also milkweed, thistle, wildflowers, and old berry canes gone dry and prickly. I have to high-step it or my shins get scratched.

But it's glorious — the wind in my hair, the golden sea of grass against the cloudless blue sky. I can't believe someone hasn't built a house up here. At the top of this hill you can see for miles: West Bay, Leelanau County, Lake Michigan again. Lake, land, lake. Blue, green, blue. My house is the third white speck north of the red speck on East Bay. I stop and take it in.

It's an awe-inspiring view. I wish Dad could see this.

I throw my head back and hold my arms out wide.

Take him, Jesus, I think. Take him. Don't make him go through any more of this. I mean it. When I get home, I hope he will have died. I really do. That is my prayer. No more suffering for him, please.

"Take him, Jesus!" I yell it out loud. "Take him!"

It feels good to say it, but it's so final, so definite, that it's scary. I'm crying now, but I shout it again.

"Take him, Jesus! Just take him!" I'm fed up with it now. "Quit messing around with my dad! Quit torturing him!"

Then I think, quit messing with whom? Quit torturing whom? Do I really mean me? Do I want Dad to die so it will finally be over and we can get on with our lives? Am I being selfish and short-sighted? A month from now, will I kick myself for wishing him gone a second sooner than he had to be?

When I get home Dad is not dead. He's praying. Alone and praying.

I duck behind the potted fig, hoping I'm hidden. Dad's not just reciting the Our Father or the Hail Mary or some prayer from a book. He's praying in his own words, out loud. Talking to Jesus like Jesus is one of his brothers. Using simple, everyday language like he really means it.

"Help me, Jesus. Help me with this pain. Give me some relief, or at least make me strong enough to bear it. To bear it in your name. Please, give me some relief from this pain. Take me up to heaven with you, Jesus. Thank you for my family, Jesus, for my wonderful wife and children. I've had a full life. Thank you for everything you've given me."

I'm shocked. I mean, Dad's always gone to church. He gets ashes on his forehead on Ash Wednesday, gives up stuff for Lent. He's even been reading the Bible lately, ever since he got sick. But I've never thought of Dad as religious.

No, I always figured he went through the motions to please

Mom and Gram, judging by the way he was always nodding off during church and slipping out right after communion to get to the golf course. And when he's mad, he swears. Not just shit or hell or damn, but the really bad ones: God damn it and Jesus Christ.

"I'm ready, Jesus. Just bless my family. Take care of them for me."

I feel so uncomfortable. This is Dad's private prayer. I shouldn't be listening. He would be so embarrassed if—

Dad looks up and sees me. "Hey, Weez, come say a prayer with me."

A made up one? In my own words? I'd feel so stupid.

"Hold my hand," says Dad.

I start saying the Our Father, and he joins me. At first I feel really awkward, but by the time we reach "Thy will be done," I'm meaning every word of it. It's the most genuine, meaningful prayer I've ever said.

So Dad is a spiritual man after all. Whether he's always been this way deep inside or whether his sickness drove him to it, it doesn't matter. Dad believes, really believes. He isn't running treadmills in his mind wondering if there's a heaven or a hell or nothing at all, wondering if there's meaning. I'm so glad. I feel so much safer knowing he's this way. And it makes it easier for me to believe, too.

CHAPTER 27

Monday, September 8

The sun-catcher crystals hanging in the window twirl slowly on their lines and send rainbows dancing across the floor.

Dad's lying here, staring up at the skylight. I'm sitting at his side, holding his hand. We aren't talking; there's nothing more to say between us, nothing a smile or a squeeze can't convey. So it's a comfortable silence.

Dad's preoccupied by something, anyway. His eyes move the way people's do when they're listening to a secret. They dart from side to side in edgy little movements, almost as if he's reading off the skylight. He's very alert. His head isn't simply resting on the pillow; he's holding his face up, his neck angled back. I look at the skylight, but all I see is blue sky.

I'm impressed by how noble he looks, how patient he's become. I wonder what he's thinking.

It's almost as if he's responding to the music Mom's playing, as if it's talking to him. The music's soft and gentle with some kind of airy whistling—a fife or a flute. Real dreamy stuff. It sounds Irish or Scottish. I've never heard it before. It's beautiful.

The song changes, grows stronger. It's sad but determined, with bagpipes moaning a heavy beat.

Dad seems to be going somewhere with it. Even though he's lying here, I sense he has embarked on a journey. It's as if someone is pulling him up out of bed by the hand, and I'm watching him go. He's a soldier being led off to war. He doesn't want to go, but it's his duty.

He's been called.

My dad is the bravest thing I've ever seen, lying there in that bed, looking up with those big, pleading eyes and those teeth so big in his thin face.

All of a sudden it looks like he's receiving something—something big. His eyes grow wide and he goes slack-jawed. It's as if he's seeing something amazing and listening to something very important.

In my mind, Dad has started up a steep stone staircase into the sky. It's narrow and winding with no railings on either side, going up so high that it tapers off into nowhere.

The music gets louder, faster, stronger. Dad's moving swiftly with it now, bounding, running, flying. All on his own. Up, up, away from us. Peacefully, resolutely, not afraid of where he's going.

I hear angels singing in the music, calling him upward, welcoming him, calming him, telling him not to be afraid. It's spooky and haunting, but the music seems to be coming straight from heaven. Dad is being shown. He's a little boy in awe, eyes full of wonder. A little boy looking up for direction and approval. "Is this right? How am I doing? Show me how. Here I am!"

I want to cheer, "Go, Pops, go!" I want him to be free.

But the way he yawns and settles his head into the pillow, I'm afraid his ascent is going to be a slow, drifting one. Quiet. Feathery and soft at times, painful and cutting at others. Strands tearing away, one by one, until he is no longer held down.

Sitting quietly at Dad's side while he sleeps, I'm surprised I'm not bored or frustrated or wishing I was somewhere else. I'm just holding his hand. Yup, Dad and I are going for the record. I don't know how long it's been now, but surely we've broken all previous records set in the Jeep. Funny how I lose all sense of time sitting here with him.

The sun's going down so it must be almost dinnertime. But I'm not hungry. I'm not anything. Which is hard to believe. I mean, I've been sitting here for hours, days, weeks, doing absolutely nothing. Except this.

I used to think, why does Dad have to get sick now, just when I've reached this huge milestone and I'm finally enjoying myself? Honestly, that's how I thought. But none of that matters now. I'll be sitting here reading the Bible to Dad to help him through a bout of pain, and I'll see he's fallen asleep on me with tears still running down his cheeks. And I'll put the Bible down and wipe the tears from his face and just sit with him, going for the record. And while I sit so quietly, I realize there's nothing else I could be doing that's as important as this. This is what life is about.

That's what I do most of the time now — sit here daydreaming. But it's not always about Dad. Sometimes when I'm zoning out, I get this picture in my mind. I don't know where it comes from, but it's of Clay.

He's in his boat, smiling his square-toothed smile, and the sun's glinting off of everything—the water, his teeth, his sunglasses, the tops of his copper curls. In the lenses of his glasses I can see the reflection of this tiny flesh-tone figure. It's too small to see if it's nude or in a bathing suit or even if it's male or female. But I think it's me.

Tuesday, September 9

"Did we get a call from Mary?" Dad's asked this at least thirty times in the last few days. It's the first thing he says when he wakes up.

"Not yet," we say.

"Poor girl. She must be about ready to pop." And he closes his eyes again.

A half hour later the clock in the living room chimes and startles him awake. "Did we get a call from Mary?"

"No."

"Poor girl," he says as Mom and I mouth it along with him. "Must be about ready to pop."

But the next time he asks we have something to tell him.

"Yes!" Mom says. "She just called. Nothing's happened yet, but she's having contractions. The doctor told her to go to the hospital."

Dad licks his lips. "Well. Let's pray everything goes well."

I grab Dad's shoulders and shake him gently. He's skin and bones. "Pops. Pops. Wake up." He's a rag doll in my hands, out stone cold. Pops," I say louder. "Pops, wake up!"

He snorts. "What? What? Mary?"

"She had her baby! It's a boy!"

"You're kidding. Where's your mother?" His eyes dart around for her as if he doesn't believe me.

"She's on the phone with Hugh."

"Did everything go all right? Are they okay?" Dad tries to lift his head off the pillow. He looks more concerned than happy.

Mom comes bursting into the sunroom. "It's a boy! Seven pounds, seven ounces, twenty-one inches long. Peter Alexander. What do you think of that, Grandpa? Peter Alexander!"

Dad's face flushes pink, but his brow stays furrowed. "And Mary? How's Mary?"

"Hugh says they're both doing fine."

Dad sinks back into his pillow and smiles. Lying there so small and gray and loose-skinned, he looks every bit a grandpa and nothing at all like my old Pops.

"Here, Pete; do you want to talk to them?" Mom hands him the phone.

"No, just tell them congratulations. Tell Hugh to have a cigar for me."

And as quickly as he woke, he drifts back to sleep.

Mom and I look at Dad's bag, then at each other.

His urine has changed. I didn't notice it this morning, but when I went to empty it after lunch, I almost threw up. I didn't say anything to Mom, given the cheer of the day, but it's obvious she's noticed it, too. How could she not? It's like the liquid in a can of kidney beans, with floating bits in it like the egg in egg drop soup.

"Do you need any Roxanol, Dad?" It's almost dinnertime and he hasn't had any since before lunch.

Dad moves his head weakly from side to side. Now that he doesn't have Mary to ask about, he's suddenly gone mute.

He stares at the skylight, his eyes going back and forth in those edgy little movements. He doesn't react to anything Mom and I say, just stays fixed on that skylight.

I keep trying to snap him out of it. "Dad, can I get you anything? Are you comfortable? Isn't it great about Mary's baby?"

He closes his eyes and acts likes he doesn't hear me.

"Leave him alone, Leah," says Mom. "Don't try to make him respond. Remember what Heather said about withdrawal?"

So we don't ask anything of Dad and he doesn't ask anything of us.

Wednesday, September 10

Mom and I have just woken up and we're sitting cross-legged, side-by-side on Mom's bed, staring at the quarter cup of kidney bean slime in Dad's bag.

"He needs to drink, Mom."

"He needs to do a lot of things, Leah."

Dad still isn't up when Heather arrives. He doesn't move when she takes his vital signs. His arm is limp as she removes the blood pressure cuff from around his shriveled biceps and takes his hand.

"Pete, can you hear me? Can you squeeze my hand? Pete?"

Heather's eyes get glassy. "I'm going to miss you, you sweet man."

She pats Dad's arm, gets up, and leads Mom by the elbow out of the room. I follow them into the kitchen.

"Rita, it's time to call Paul and Mary home."

"But Mary just had her baby yesterday!"

Heather raises her eyebrows. "These things are never convenient. You might be able to wait a day or two."

"We'll wait, then. I don't want to worry her. She isn't even home from the hospital yet. And how can I call Paul and not Mary?"

Mom lowers her head into her hands. Heather puts an arm around her.

"It's like he was waiting," says Mom, wiping her eyes. She's gotten so good at pulling herself together quickly. "Like he was hanging on for the baby to be born. The change has been so dramatic. Overnight. It must have taken more than I realized, and he just didn't have anything left."

"Yes," says Heather, "we see this a lot. Patients have a big milestone, a date they set for themselves. More patients die the day after Christmas than any other day of the year."

"I don't get it," I say. "Doesn't he want to see the baby? Isn't that something to hang on for? It's only another week or so."

"Oh, sure, honey, but there are so many things to hang on for," says Mom. "There's our anniversary at the end of the month, the holidays, seeing you off to college. And there's no way he can make all of them. It's probably a miracle he was able to hang on until the baby was born."

Maybe. But it seems to me this baby, his first grandchild, would be something to celebrate, not something to make him quit trying and let go.

Now that it looks like we may be near the end I'm getting stubborn again. This just can't happen.

CHAPTER 28

Thursday, September 11

"The time has come for my departure. I have fought the good fight, I have finished the race, I have kept the faith . . ." I'm reading Dad's favorite Bible passage to him, 2 Timothy 4:6-8.

He hasn't opened his eyes or spoken in two days. He startles every now and then, and we turn him several times a day so he won't get bedsores, but other than that, he doesn't move.

Mom says we have to keep talking to him and reading to him.

". . . Now there is in store for me the crown of righteousness, which the Lord, the righteous Judge, will award to me on that day."

Dad chokes, snorts, and gags. He's breathing in fits and starts, like a backfiring car about to stall. I wonder if it's the death rattle everybody talks about. But then he settles into a rhythm again.

A sharp clattering of metal breaks the silence, and Mom and I look up from our books. Dad's hands are clamped onto the top bars of the side rails, his knuckles white and trembling. He looks like he's sleeping, except his brow is lifted in that helpless, pained expression, the way saints always look in paintings and books.

Mom pries his near hand off the metal bar and holds it. "Its okay, Pete. It's okay. I'm right here. Leah, go get some Roxanol."

I run to the kitchen, wondering how we're going to get him to drink it, wondering who will hold his head back and who will pour it in his mouth and if he'll choke on it and cough and sputter it in our faces like he did last time.

"Here, Mom."

She doesn't take it.

"Here, Mom." I nudge her with my wrist.

She shakes her head.

"What?"

Her head drops and she starts kissing Dad's hand, over and over. Her shoulders are bouncing up and down. She's crying, but she's not breathing.

Neither is Dad, I realize. His other hand slips off the bar. Mom is sobbing now; huge heaving sobs rack her body.

Oh, my God, Dad is dead. I think he's dead.

Mom puts her arm around me and draws me in.

Dad's chest isn't rising or falling, but something more than that is different about him. I've never believed in vibes, never felt anyone's aura, but Dad's is gone, no doubt about it. He's empty. This is just his shell we're staring at.

Is this all there is to it?

I didn't get to kiss him or hold his hand or say a prayer with him. I wasn't even here at his side! Is this all I get? Some eventless passing? A person can die with no more ceremony than it takes to tie a shoe or yawn or turn on the TV?

Mom's crying, her head buried in Dad's chest, and all I can think is, "So what do we do now?" Call Heather? Call an ambulance? A funeral home?

"Go get your grandma," says Mom.

Gram's head is back against her chair, but her lips are moving and she's fingering her rosary.

"Gram."

She opens her eyes. " Sweetie?"

I can't say it. "Come with me, Gram."

She doesn't ask why. One look at my face and she flings her rosary onto the bed and follows me.

Mom moves aside for Gram.

Gram touches Dad's arm and her breath catches. She recoils her hand up to her mouth, covering it lightly. Her eyes go squinty and she looks at Mom, terrified, unbelieving—really?

Gram makes the sign of the cross over herself, folds her hands in prayer, and closes her eyes. When she opens them, she bends down and puts her hands on either side of Dad's temples and kisses him on the forehead. Her boy. Her Petey.

She's not crying. Neither am I.

"Should I call Paul and Mary?" I ask Mom.

"Yes, would you, please? Paul will know what to do."

I mean to go do it, but somehow I can't. I don't want to leave Dad. It's like his death will be over then. Like he will be over. Shouldn't I say goodbye somehow? Shouldn't I hug him or kiss him or hold his hand? But I've no more desire to do that than to kiss a stone wall.

I back slowly out of the room. I guess that's it. I guess he's dead, and now we get on with things.

Saturday, September 13

I'm not crying. I should be, but I'm not.

Dad's in a casket wearing his navy suit that's ten sizes too big for him now. The undertaker did a terrible job on him. His lips look funny. They're all tight over his teeth like they've been sewn together. And his hair—he never wore it like that! I should go ruffle it up.

No, I better stay here, in the middle of the room where I can talk to people as they file past to see Dad. Mom says that's what we're supposed to do. We have to give people privacy when they're up by Dad.

But I want to go up there now. I want to fix Dad's hair.

Everybody's here. Mary, Hugh, the baby. Dad's family, Mom's family. Enzo. People Dad's done business with. Golf buddies. Regulars from the bar. Old friends from Milwaukee. Neighbors. People from church and school, teachers, Mr. Pfieffer, my whole high school soccer team.

Over in the corner by the door there's this group of kids. They look like they're afraid. They've probably never seen a dead person before, and they're not sure what they're supposed to do. Mandy, Kristin, Rebe, Sam, Jake, Clay . . .

Clay!

I bolt over to him and hug him. Hard. He pries me loose and grabs my hand and leads me out into the hall. He's practically dragging me.

There's this nook in the wall, a little telephone booth with folding doors. He pulls me in and shuts the door.

He puts his arms around me. He's holding me up. I dissolve into a snotty mess, all those tears for Dad that I've been holding in finally pouring out. My face is pressed into Clay's shoulder, and he doesn't seem to care that his clothes are getting slimed.

As we stand there hugging, I think, how did he know exactly what I would want?" If I had a clear mind, that is. How did he know I really didn't want to stand there in public with everyone seeing me hug him?

Clay's crying, too. I can feel him shake. It makes me cry even harder, but in a way it makes me feel happy, too.

Why does this feel so good? Would a hug from anybody else feel as good? Or is it just human touch? Has it been that long since I've allowed anybody to touch me? I mean really touch me—not just standing stiffly while somebody hugs me—but where I've actually sought it out and given in to it?

Or does it feel so good because it's Clay who's hugging me? He's so warm and his shoulders are so . . .

I push off his chest. "I'm okay now."

But am I? My face is burning up. Good thing it's dark in here.

Organ music starts playing, so it must be time for the wake ceremony. I push the door open, grab Clay's hand, and pull him back into the room. Everyone's taking a seat in the rows of wooden fold-up chairs. My family's seated in the front.

All of a sudden I don't care what anybody thinks—I want Clay to sit by me. I don't let go of his hand. I pull him down the center aisle, in front of everybody, and we sit next to Mom. She looks over and smiles at us, but I keep holding his hand.

CHAPTER 29

Friday, September 19

Everyone has gone home and left Mom and me on our own for the first time since Dad died. Even Gram's gone away for a while, to Milwaukee to be with her boys.

I'm a zombie, sitting here slouched on the couch, waiting for Mom. She's in her bedroom getting ready. She says she has to go to the bank.

Mom comes down the hall dressed real sharp: blazer, pants, blouse, all her usual noisy jewelry. She's curled her hair and she's wearing lipstick, eyeliner, her pearly pink nail polish.

I don't know why it strikes me as weird. Except for the last few days, it's how she always looks. So Dad's dead and life goes on; is that how it is for her? She can bounce back that quickly? Not me. I've got bags under my eyes, I've been wearing the same sweats three days in a row, and I don't care.

"What?" says Mom.

"Nothing. You look nice."

"Thank you. I thought it might make me feel better to freshen up."

"Come on, Mom. I'll drive." I might as well get some practice, now that my chauffeur's gone.

I'm numb walking out to the car. I feel like I've just stepped off a plane. Everything's muffled. The sun hurts my eyes. My head aches.

Behind her sunglasses Mom looks dead, too. Her eyes are cloudy and dull, her face expressionless.

I drop Mom off in front of the bank. "I'll park and wait for you in the car."

"Okay, I shouldn't be long. I just want to see if I can cash in one of our CDs to pay off the funeral. We get a better deal if we pay within seven days."

I park and put my head back and fall asleep. Next thing I know Mom is knocking on the window. It feels like she's been gone a long time. I had this complicated dream about everyone in our family. Dad was there, too, and he didn't have cancer.

I want Mom to go away so I can go back to sleep and continue the dream.

"Where now?" I ask.

"We need food, but I don't feel like grocery shopping."

"Home?"

"No, not there either."

"The beach, then. Let's go to the beach."

"Okay."

We lay in the sand where the beach slants up into a bank beneath the grass-line. The sand is warm against my back. I don't know about Mom, but I've been cold. For the past week, I've been so cold.

"It feels so good to rest my eyes," says Mom. "The sun never stops shining, does it?"

"I guess not." Even when it seems like it should.

"We're in no hurry. Let's enjoy the sun. Take a nap if you want."

I close my eyes, but tired as I am, I can't sleep. My mind keeps churning. Not on any one thought, but in a hundred directions. Mostly on memories, flashbacks from last weekend when everyone was here. Clay. Gram. The uncles. Mary.

I'm not sad right now, just numb. Too tired to direct my thoughts, I'm drifting, floating listlessly along on the breeze. My eyelids are warm. I see yellow. Orangeish-yellow. I give in to the sand, limp. I can't feel my hands or my legs, can't picture what position I'm in. My body feels heavy, like it's sinking.

I don't know if I'm awake or asleep anymore, and I don't care.

Monday, September 22

Mom says I have to go back to school today. She shakes a finger at me as she pulls me into the kitchen for breakfast. "You can't stay home all year. You've got to go back sometime. It'll be hard no matter when you do it, Leah."

She thinks I don't want to go, but I do. She's the reason I've been staying home. I can't wait to get out of this house with all its constant reminders of Dad. Everything I look at in here makes me cry. I'm so tired of crying.

I want to see Clay, stop at his locker, eat lunch with him. We've got calculus and AP Chem together. He's what's kept me sane this past week.

The only thing I'm worried about is everybody assuming

I'm ready to play soccer again.

I'm not.

Clay is the first to ask. He comes up to me at my locker. "So, you going to practice tonight? Pffiefer's going to be glad to have you back, that's for sure."

"No."

"No, what?"

I slam my locker door shut. "No, as in N-O. No, I'm not going."

"Why not?"

"I don't want to play anymore."

"What? Why not?"

"I've got some issues there."

"Issues?"

How do I begin to explain? "Clay, a lot of things happened during that time we weren't seeing each other."

"I guess."

"I didn't just quit playing because I wanted to be at home with my dad. I quit because I was disgusted with myself. My dad's getting sick, it really woke me up." I bow my head and pinch my nose.

Clay pulls me into the empty gym and we sit on the bleachers. He waits until I collect myself, then he asks, "What do you mean—it woke you up?"

"Well, here I've spent all this time thinking soccer is so important, making my parents' lives revolve around it—weekends, mealtimes, vacations—and then when I finally get to where I've been aiming, I see it for what it is: a game. A stupid, over-hyped game. Nothing, absolutely zero, in the grand scheme of things. And it took losing my dad to put it into perspective.

"I was taking him for granted, taking my whole family for granted and putting them second to soccer. I mean, before my dad got sick, when did I ever thank them for anything? They fed me, took care of me, bought me clothes, and what did I do? I asked for more. Drive me here, drive me there, get me some Gatorade, wash my uniform. I was such a spoiled brat. Maybe I got what I deserved."

"Cut it out, Leah. It isn't your fault. People die. You can't blame yourself. Loving soccer doesn't make you evil. Your mom and dad loved it, too. They wanted to do those things for you. If you were such a burden, your dad would have let you know, in no uncertain terms."

I smile. Clay's right. Dad would never be anybody's silent servant. It's just that I need someone to blame, and I'm the only person I can find.

"I still feel sick about it. I got caught up in it and lost touch. It's like a cult. There's this whole inner circle of people you aspire to be with, big name coaches and players. Pele and Austin Gillingham and Mia Hamm. And the lingo; it's almost spiritual! Coaches talk about passion, dedication, giving your heart and soul, how your team is your family. What do those ads say? 'It's not just a game; it's life.'"

Clay's looking at me like I'm crazy.

"It's all about ego. You dream of seeing your name in the

headlines, of giving an interview, of playing in a stadium with thousands of people cheering. It's so vain. You're trying to look good so you'll impress some coach, so you'll intimidate the player who's got to mark you. All that matters is your body. How do I look? Am I fit? Am I cut? How do I feel? Tired? Sore? Thirsty? It's like you're a fine-tuned machine and you're always checking your gauges. 'Oh, good God!'" I use my hairy conniption voice. "'It's two hours until match time! I should've eaten my pre-game meal by now!'"

Clay laughs. "I know. Whatever happened to being a little kid and wolfing down a Happy Meal a half an hour before the match? No stretching, no warming up, you just run out there and play with a belly full of Coke and fries."

I slap my thighs. "Yes! That's what I'm saying! It used to be so simple. But then I got so caught up in it. Clay, I can honestly tell you that in the past four years, I have cared about nothing else. Nothing. And I used to be proud of that."

Clay's nodding his head knowingly, and it's aggravating me. This is supposed to be my confession, something he knows nothing about.

"So what are you going to do?" he asks. "Just give up soccer? Bag college and the Olympics and everything you've worked for?"

"I don't know. Probably. At least for now."

Clay shakes his head and stares down between his knees. "Wow. You're right. You've got issues."

CHAPTER 30

Monday, September 29

I see Mr. Pfieffer got smart to the boys. He put up a dark green windscreen on the fence between the two fields. No more checking out the babes whenever they feel like it. I'm glad. It was so distracting how they'd stand around during their water break staring at us.

I sit under the bleachers waiting for Clay to come out of the locker room. I usually go to the library and do my homework while Clay's at practice, and then we go get something to eat. But I got bored today and left early. I suppose I'm no better than those gawking boys, hiding out under the bleachers, watching Clay.

I climb out. The boys are all gone, so I cross their field and go over to take a peek at the girls through one of the flap holes in the wind netting.

They're still out on the field, running sprints. The new freshman is really fast—what's her name—Zoe? And there's Jenna, the one who took my—

Ka-ching! A ball hits the chain link fence a couple feet from my head. It's Clay.

"Caught you peeking!" he yells across the field.

Shh, I motion to him, shooting a finger to my lips.

He's chuckling at me as he walks up, shaking his head. "Come on, Leah, it's time you got back to playing. It'd be good for you."

"No, it wouldn't."

"Yes, it would. It would make your life feel more normal. You just were telling me how there isn't one thing that feels normal since your dad died. Well, that's because a big part of your life is missing, besides your dad. Come on, what would he want you to do?"

"Play, probably."

"There you go. He'd want you to play. And so do I. Isn't that enough?"

Maybe Clay's right. He usually is. Maybe I'd get out there and love it all over again. I doubt it, but . . .

"Okay, I'll give it a try, but only because—"

Clay gives me a hug and picks me up off the ground.

"All right! My Weasel is back!"

Friday, October 3

Leland's pre-game warm-up tape blares over the loudspeakers. A group of little Leland girls wave purple and gold pompoms. People are talking and laughing in the bleachers, mothers dancing their babies to the music.

What's the matter with you? I want to shout at them all. Don't you know my dad just died? How can people be so happy? It's so disrespectful.

Mrs. Holleran and another woman walk by on the sidelines, each carrying a cardboard tray loaded with hot dogs and drinks. Mrs. Holleran spots me and twinkle toes over to the field where I'm stretching.

"Leah, honey, I'm so sorry about your dad." She gives me mournful eyes and squeezes my arm. "Is your mom here?"

"No, she's at a meeting." A meeting for people who've lost their spouses. Her first one. I didn't want her to miss it, so I didn't tell her about today's game.

"Well, tell her I say hi. It's really great to have you back."

Coach Pfieffer pulls me aside. "Leah, I know this is your first game back, but I think it's best to get you going right away. I'm having you start. Even if you're not one hundred percent, we need you in there. Ready?"

I shrug.

The ref's whistle blows, and it's like I never left. Kristin the foghorn is hollering at us nonstop. Mr. Pfieffer's down on one knee, chewing his gum like mad. And I've got the same tired, burnt-out feeling I had when I left. Only it's worse now, because I'm so out of shape.

I wonder if it shows in my play.

Don't worry, you'll get your second wind, I tell myself.

But I don't.

It wouldn't be so bad if all the girls weren't looking for me. But every run I make, no matter where I go, they give me the ball. It's like they're trying to be nice to me. But I can't do anything with it once I get it. Just running to it takes everything I've got and then I have to pass off and curl wide for a rest.

I pat my chest as I run by the bench. My lungs are on fire.

Coach Pffiefer must not be getting the message.

"Coach!" I yell as I rainbow in front of our bench again. "I need out."

He shakes his head and puts an index finger up. "Give it another minute. "Yes? Can you?"

No. I shake my head no. I stop running, bend over, and put my hands on my knees. I hang my head and refuse to budge.

"Jenna!" Coach shouts. "Get in there for Leah."

From the bench, it looks even more foolish. Soccer. Scoring goals. The girls with their jersey sleeves rolled up so they won't get a farmer's tan. Mr. Holleran yelling at the referees, all red in the face over a stupid game.

Mr. Pfieffer gathers us in a circle at halftime and launches into his pep talk. It's the same talk that drove me away the last time.

"Ladies, we're not into this game. We're not playing with any of this." He thumps his chest. "Have some pride. Get fired up."

Blah, blah, blah.

I look around at the other girls. They're eating this stuff up, staring earnestly at Coach Pfieffer, faces all serious. They hang their heads when he yells and nod in agreement.

It's so hard to sit here with everyone all gung-ho and intense. I just want to laugh at them and yell, Wake up, guys! It's just a game. There are more important things to worry about.

A curtain goes down in my brain. For the first time in my life, I feel like a cynic. I hate being this way, but come on, what's the big deal? So what if we lose? I mean really. So what?

Before we take the field for the second half, we huddle to pile our hands and cheer "Let's-Go-Trojans." As captains, my hands and Kristin's are supposed to be the first two out. I'll feel like a hypocrite laying mine down on top of Kristin's and pretending I'm into this team effort, but everybody's waiting for me, so I do it.

Two minutes into the half I'm wheezing. My throat's so tight a pea would get stuck going down. I can't breathe. I bend over. I stand up. I look around and find Clay in the stands. I run off the field as fast as I can and head straight for the parking lot.

I'm bent over the back of Clay's car trying to breathe through my tiny, bunched-up throat when I feel Clay's hand on my shoulder.

"Why am I breathing like this?"

"You're hyperventilating, Leah."

"But is it because I'm out of shape, or because I'm upset, or because I'm upset that I'm out of shape? Or am I upset and out of shape, but the upset part is about Dad? Because I don't think I care what kind of shape I'm in anymore." I've got no breath, but I'm talking like an auctioneer.

"Shh, Leah, shh. Just catch your breath."

"Let's get out of here. Please, take me home. I just want to go home."

"Your bag. You left it on the field."

"I don't care. Let's just go. I'm not going back."

He unlocks the car and I jump in.

"It's okay," says Clay. "It's just too soon is all. Your emotions are still raw. In another couple weeks you'll be ready to go back."

"No, I won't. I'm not playing soccer anymore."

"Leah, don't talk foolish. Soccer's your life. You've put so much into it. You've got so much to look forward to."

"No, Clay. I quit. Forget college, the Olympics, and everything else."

"Your dad would want you to keep playing."

Would he? In his newly divine wisdom, would Dad still think soccer is so important, or is he laughing right now and shaking his head at the foolishness of it all?

When we're out of the parking lot Clay reaches over and holds my hand. For a second it feels good, but then it reminds me of going for the record with Dad, and I pull it away.

Clay flips his head to the side. I've hurt his feelings again. I scoot over next to him and put my head on his shoulder. I don't really want to—it's such a girlfriend thing to do—but I want him to know that it's not him.

When I get home, Mom's not back from her meeting yet, and I'm glad.

"Want to come in, Clay?"

"Sure."

"Raid the fridge, Clay. I'm going to go take these sweaty clothes off."

I try to pull my jersey over my head, but it gets caught up in the T-shirt underneath and nearly chokes me. Separating the shirts, I spot myself in the mirror, standing there holding the jersey up and the T-shirt down.

WTIPSWBTBWI: the letters look aggravatingly the same backward as they do frontward. I yank the shirts off, one after the other, the neck of the T-shirt ripping as it catches going over my nose.

"Clay," I yell from my bedroom, "I don't think it's a good idea for you to be over here after all. My mom might be home any minute now."

"I thought we'd gotten beyond that, Leah."

"We have." How do I tell him to get lost? "Clay, I just want to be alone right now. I know my moods must be hard to understand. It's not you, though."

The minute he leaves, I run out to the deck with the sweaty old rag of a T-shirt. I lift the lid to the grill, squirt charcoal lighter across the letters, and throw a match on it. FOOM! The letters bubble and sizzle and curl up on themselves. The yellow fabric turns brown and then black as the fire spreads, leaving only the stink of plastic in its wake.

There.

I go back to my room to undress the rest of the way, and there it is, waiting, staring me flat in the face: my Wall of Fame.

Wall of Fame. How full of myself I've been. I can't look at it without wincing.

It's got to come down, all of it.

One by one, I pull them off their nails: the plaques, the medals, the trophies, the framed certificates. Then I climb up on my desk chair and clear the shelf of trophies. A clean sweep. I pile

200

them all on the floor, throw my dirty uniform over the heap, and dash into the bathroom.

After my shower I'll take it all out to the garbage.

CHAPTER 31

Saturday, October 4

After weeks of sitting idle, my running shoes are crisp and curled up at the toes like elf boots. I lean over to tie my laces and feel a tweak at the back of each leg.

My muscles are sore. I love this feeling, almost forgot what it's like, that small ache when you stretch. I used to think it was a sign of growing stronger.

Yeah, despite the nightmare of my comeback attempt yesterday, I realize one thing: I miss exercising. So I'm going to start running again. Today I'm going up to the cemetery, two miles there, two miles back. I go there everyday anyway; I might as well run.

Standing at Dad's grave, I feel hollow, emotionless, cold as stone. I can't even bring myself to cry. I don't know why I do this. He's not here. It's just his body under there. Just a bunch of bones and diseased tissue.

It's a respect thing, I guess. That, and I like to read his name on the stone. To know that he lived. I like that other people will see it, too, and that they'll see Mom's name beside his and know that he was loved.

I never stay long.

Mom's sitting at the dining room table, writing thank-you notes. It's all she does these days. She's written hundreds of them.

I sit on the floor beside her to stretch. "Aren't you sick of doing that?"

"No, actually I'm not. It's kind of therapeutic. It gives me something to do."

"I wish I had something worthwhile to do."

Mom looks down at me. "You do. You're going to school, seeing friends, playing soccer. You just went running."

"Yeah, but none of it means anything."

"How can you say that? You love doing those things."

"But I don't feel any purpose. I need a goal. I need something I can get really fired up about."

"What about soccer?"

"Nah, it's not the same. I'm just not into it anymore."

Mom's eyebrows bunch together. I'm not sure I want to explain it to her. I definitely don't want to hear I told you so right now.

"You know, Mom, how some of the things you used to worry about suddenly seemed so unimportant once Dad got sick?"

She nods.

"It's like we spent so much time with Dad, reading the Bible, talking about life and what really matters, that now I go around separating the trivial things from the things that are truly worthwhile—in everything I do! I can't help it. And so much of what I used to do seems totally unimportant in the big picture. I hear kids at school talking about clothes, hair, parties, and it makes me sick."

"I know what you mean, Leah. It's like I've got one foot in this world and one foot in the next. It's hard to join the living again, isn't it?"

For once Mom and I see eye to eye on something.

"But you've got a lot of living left to do, Leah, and so do I. It's not wrong to enjoy things. There's so much beauty in this world, so much God put here for us to enjoy."

"I know, Mom, it's just that I have no sense of purpose. I want to bounce out of bed like I used to, all fired up, knowing exactly what I was aiming to accomplish that day. I wonder if I'll ever feel a drive like that again."

"You will. It's just going to take some time. Don't be so hard on yourself."

"But I'm used to having a goal; if I don't find one soon, I'm going to go crazy."

"Have a little patience while you work things out. Something will come to you."

"I was thinking, maybe I could volunteer in a soup kitchen or a homeless shelter. Or join Big Brothers/Big Sisters."

"Those are all fine ideas, Leah. You can go to college and get an education towards any number of service related professions. You could be a doctor, a counselor, a teacher."

"No, Mom, I need something I can do now. I don't want to waste anymore time. I want to make a difference now."

Sunday, October 5

All through church I think about it. What can I do? What really matters?

I could tutor kids after school. I could join a cause like Habitat for Humanity or Save The Rainforest or Save the Whales.

I think of all the people I know, all their jobs, and all the volunteer work they do. And then it comes to me: Heather, the job she has, how much it meant to Dad and us to have her there caring for him.

I want to do what Heather does.

When we get home from church, I call the Maple Valley Nursing Home. A woman answers.

"Hi, my name is Leah Weiczynkowski. I'm a senior at Senior High and I'd like to volunteer." It comes rolling off my tongue just as I rehearsed it.

"We can always use volunteers," the woman says. "When would you be available?"

Monday, October 6

I walk through the doors and smell urine. A hundred other clean, piney, lemony odors try to cover it up, but it's there underneath it all.

And the quiet. The weird, empty quiet. The hallway vibrates with it.

All those old people. Rounded backs. Wheelchairs. Hospital beds. Tubes and bags. Gaping mouths. Vacant stares. Big ears, big noses. Sunken cheeks. Liver spots. That waxy white skin, paper thin, tinged blue and yellow.

All these old, dying people, shuffling around. Every time I look at one, I see Dad. Dad, in a different bathrobe.

And that's what I'm trying to get rid of. This image of Dad as sick and old. Every time I picture him, he's weak and thin like he was this summer.

I stop and close my eyes. I go through my files, shuffling through the snapshots to get to the one I want: my tan, thick-middled, smiling dad, dressed to a tee, standing erect, wearing his photo grays.

"Excuse me."

An old man with a walker is bumping towards me, and all my snapshots flutter away like cards in a game of fifty-two-pickup.

I'm standing in the middle of the hallway. "Oh, sorry." Stepping out of his way, I try to smile at him, but I can't.

A lump forms in my throat, and I grab the handrail on the wall.

I can't do this.

I turn around and walk out before I even get to the check-in desk.

CHAPTER 32

Tuesday, October 7

"Leah," Mom yells from the other end of the house, "have you vacuumed the sunroom?" We're doing some serious housecleaning for the first time since Dad died. A very fun after-school activity.

"No, not yet," I yell back.

Doesn't she know we lose thousands of skin cells and hundreds of hairs every day? Dad lay here for months, falling apart. There must be plenty of him still lying around on the floor in here. And I'm supposed to suck it all up? It seems so sad not to leave some trace of him. Wouldn't it be comforting, years from now, to take your socks off at night and see a curly gray Einstein hanging from one of them?

Not an hour, not a half hour, not fifteen minutes goes by that I don't think about him.

Sometimes I bury my nose in the armpits of his suits still hanging in the closet and wallow in his good musky smell.

I sit down on the canister vacuum, elbows on my knees, chin in hands. It's just too hard to believe that I'll never see him again on this earth.

I have dreams that he comes back to us. Not like Jesus and

the resurrection; no, he just walks into the house one day, brought back to life and cured by modern medicine. And we're never shocked to see him. It's more like, "Dad! I'm so glad you're back. Thank goodness for technology."

"Leah!" Mom shouts again. I turn on the vacuum, drowning her out, hopefully shutting her up. I stay on the vacuum holding the wand in the air so as not to suck up any precious stuff.

Speaking of dreams, I'm waiting for a vision or a sign from Dad, one that will let me know he's okay and that he's watching over me. I do things to make him proud, things I wouldn't bother doing if I didn't feel like he was watching so I know I have a definite sense of his being out there somewhere.

I have to believe that he's out there, that he's not just gone. In science we learned nothing can be created or destroyed; it only changes form. I know there's that whole thing about from dust we come, to dust we return, but I'm not talking about his body. I'm talking about his spirit, his soul. It's somewhere, in some form, and that form is not dirt. I want to know where it went, what it became, and how I can feel it again.

Because right now I'm just feeling this huge void. I'm numb. I don't feel like eating or watching TV or reading or going outside. All I can think to do is sleep and make the time pass faster—because as people are always saying—time heals. I doubt anything can heal this, but I've got no choice but to give it a shot.

Gram says it never goes away, the void, but that it eventually does stop hurting. She should know. She's been through a lot of deaths: her mom and dad, a brother, two sisters, a husband, a son. So I talk to her about it a lot.

I think I'll go call her right now. I turn off the vacuum and take the cordless phone into my room.

Gram answers. "Yello?"

"Green," I say.

"Oh, you!" Gram growls at my teasing of the way she says hello; I always answer red or green or blue. "So it's you, Sweetie. How's your mom doing?"

"Eh."

"Well, you be strong for her."

"I will."

"So what's the occasion?"

"Nothing. I just wanted to talk to you."

"Well, it's good to hear your voice. I miss youse."

"We miss you, too."

"So tell me what's new."

"I'm going to start working at the restaurant after school and on weekends."

"Your pa would like that. Maybe you can take over for him someday."

"Ha."

"How's school going?"

"Good. All right. Not great. Gram, I try to keep busy, but it's like I'm constantly bored. I try to fill up my time with anything and everything, but nothing works. I don't think working at the restaurant is going to help either."

"Sweetie, stop trying to fill it up. I told you, the void never goes away. You can't make it go away. You shouldn't want it to go away."

"What?"

"That's your pa's place in your heart, that void. It will always be there. No one and nothing can ever take his place. Don't think of it as this empty hole you've got to fill. Keep it as a special place you can go to, a place full of memories. Let it stay open and don't be afraid to visit it; that's your sacred place. Go there when you miss him, when you want to feel close to him."

Gee, I never knew Gram was so warm and fuzzy.

"But still, I wish I could find something worthwhile to do with my life, Gram. Something really noble, really important in the grand scheme of things."

"You know what Mother Theresa said, 'We cannot do great things on this earth. We can only do small things with great love.'"

When I get off the phone, I lie on my bed and think about all the things Gram said. I think long and hard.

I like her way of thinking about the void. Leaving it be, keeping it as this secret spot to go to. It would be a relief, too, if I could stop trying to fill it, because nothing's working.

And that Mother Theresa quote. Maybe I won't ever do any great humanitarian deed, but if I do every little thing all day long the best I can, if I say good morning like I mean it, and smile at everyone I meet, and open doors for people, maybe that's enough. Maybe I will leave this world a better place.

CHAPTER 33

Friday, October 17

I scrape plate after plate of coleslaw into the garbage. It's Fish-'n'-Chips Night at the restaurant, and I reek. Last Friday when Clay picked me up, he pinched his nose and drove real fast all the way home, saying he didn't want his leather soaking up the smell. He was kidding, but when I got home I really noticed it. It was even in my hair.

Enzo comes bursting through the swinging doors. He's always checking up on me, like I'm a china doll that might crack.

"How's it going?" he yells over the sprayers. "How's my clean-up crew?"

I grab him by the elbow on his sweep through to the kitchen. "Enzo, can I please graduate from clean-up crew to waitress?"

Enzo's good to me, but sometimes I feel like Cinderella. I used to be the owner's daughter; now I'm begging to get out of scrubbing pots and pans.

Enzo shakes his head. "For all your grace on the soccer field, you got the touch of an elephant with a tray in your hand."

It's true. I've broken a lot of glasses.

"But practice makes perfect, right? How am I going to get better if you never let me do it?"

Enzo scrunches up his face. He knows I've got a point.

"Okay. I'll give you five o'clock to six o'clock, Monday nights. But that's it until you show me you can handle a tray."

Enzo comes back about a half hour later and says in a real low voice, "Leah, will you do me a really big favor?"

"Sure, what?"

"The boys and I are trying to round up enough people for our match tomorrow, but it's a strange weekend. Everyone's out of town for one reason or another, and we're one player shy of eleven-a-side. Will you play with us?"

"Enzo."

Anything but that.

"Please," he begs. "What else have you got going? Come on; you can be on my team." He flashes me his most charming grin.

I know how much his Saturday matches mean to him. "Enzo, I haven't played in weeks. You wouldn't want me on your team, believe me."

"Leah, even in your most out-of-shape state, you're still three steps ahead of a bunch of old men."

"Enzo."

"Come on. You of all people should know how I hate to miss a chance to play."

"Okay, but just this once," I say. "Don't ever ask me to do this again."

Saturday, October 18

Enzo and the other guys don't treat me like a girl when we're on the field. No, these guys go hard. They joke around and are good sports about everything, but they want to win.

It's fun. No pressure. No ego. Well, a little bit of ego, but it's the right kind. It's like it used to be—just plain fun. Soccer for soccer's sake. I'm not the best player out here, either. There are some young guys, strong and fast and quick. And the older guys might be out of shape, but they're skilled and smart, life-long students of the game, like Enzo.

It feels good. The soft tap, tap, tap of the ball at my feet as I dribble. I'm surprised. It's like riding a bike. I didn't forget how to play. I'm a little slow, but my touch is there.

Enzo's on my team and he keeps trying to set me up.

I make a run far post, and he slots me a pass that's right on the money. I fake the shot, take two touches to the side, and unload on the ball. It sails into the upper right corner.

An electric surge passes through me as it tickles the net. I feel this joy well up in me, this foreign and nearly forgotten thrill. I feel guilty for feeling it, but it's too simple to be anything but good.

I want to jump and hoot and pump my fists. It's so satisfying to score a goal! One simple little goal. I'd forgotten what a charge it gives you.

It's starting to rain, but we keep playing. I slide tackle, and when I get up the whole right side of my body is streaked green and brown. The backs of everyone's legs are splattered with mud. We're slipping and sliding. The ball drags through a puddle in a low spot, spraying water as it rolls. Three people are whacking at it, unable to get their footing. I laugh at the foolishness of the scene. This is war, down and dirty. Only the tough survive. We look like wet rats.

I hope the game doesn't get called on account of lightning. I'm having too much fun.

I don't even know who wins, the game was such a mess. But Enzo looks happy coming off the field, so it might have been us.

We exchange a muddy handshake. "Thanks, Enzo. That was fun."

"Good. You look like you picked up right where you left off. I knew this was all it would take to get you back to it."

He knew this was all it would take? To get me back to it?

I look around, and sure enough, there's Clay. Sitting in his car, in the parking lot next to the field.

I cock my head to the side. "Enzo?"

"What?" He pleads innocence with his hands, but he's smirking.

I run over to Clay's car, and just as I expected, he's wearing this impish grin, all proud of himself.

I open the passenger door and get in, muddy shorts and all. "I suppose you're going to tell me you just happened to be driving by and you saw me playing and thought you'd stop to see what I'm up to." I punch him in the arm. "I should have known you were behind this."

He's holding his bicep and rubbing it—I really nailed him—but he's still got that smile smeared all over his face. "It wasn't my idea."

"Right."

"Really."

"Whose was it, then?"

"Your mom's."

Mom. My nose prickles.

"She asked me if I could come up with a way to get you back out on the field."

"Thank you," I say. "And I'm sorry."

I hope he knows I mean it.

"For what?"

I reach for his hand and he flinches like I'm going to slug him again.

"For everything."